"*Dannie likes it here,*"

Connor said, wondering immediately why he couldn't be more subtle.

"Of course she does. What's not to like? Sun, surf, trees, horses . . ."

"Me."

"You especially. You aren't what I would have expected from . . . someone like you."

"What's *someone like me*?" Shifting into a Southern drawl, he protested, "I'm just a plain country boy, honey. I do a little pickin' an' singin' is all. It's perfectly possible for someone you know to suddenly become someone everybody knows about. With us it just happened in reverse. Now you know I'm human."

Too human. Suddenly she was in his arms, meeting his kiss with the full measure of her need.

Dear Reader:

Romance offers us all so much. It makes us "walk on sunshine." It gives us hope. It takes us out of our own lives, encouraging us to reach out to others. Janet Dailey is fond of saying that romance is a state of mind, that it could happen anywhere. Yet nowhere does romance seem to be as good as when it happens *here*.

Starting in February 1986, Silhouette Special Edition is featuring the AMERICAN TRIBUTE—a tribute to America, where romance has never been so wonderful. For six consecutive months, one out of every six Special Editions will be an episode in the AMERICAN TRIBUTE, a portrait of the lives of six women, all from Oklahoma. Look for the first book, *Love's Haunting Refrain* by Ada Steward, as well as stories by other favorites—Jeanne Stephens, Gena Dalton, Elaine Camp and Renee Roszel. You'll know the AMERICAN TRIBUTE by its patriotic stripe under the Silhouette Special Edition border.

AMERICAN TRIBUTE—six women, six stories, starting in February.

AMERICAN TRIBUTE—one of the reasons Silhouette Special Edition is just that—Special.

The Editors at Silhouette Books

KATHLEEN EAGLE
Georgia Nights

Silhouette Special Edition

Published by Silhouette Books New York

America's Publisher of Contemporary Romance

For Mary, my mother, whom I have always loved,
and for her special friendship with Jean,
whose determined efforts on behalf of her son
became a front line onslaught
in the battle for special education.

SILHOUETTE BOOKS
300 East 42nd St., New York, N.Y. 10017

Copyright © 1986 by Kathleen Eagle

ISBN: 0-373-09304-7

First Silhouette Books printing April 1986

America's Publisher of Contemporary Romance

Printed in the U.S.A.

KATHLEEN EAGLE

is both a writer and a teacher whose experiences in each profession continue to enrich her enjoyment of the other. She is presently serving as president of the North Dakota Council of Teachers of English, and has discovered that giving up doing what she liked least left more time for family, friends and writing the stories she really wants to tell. She gave up housework.

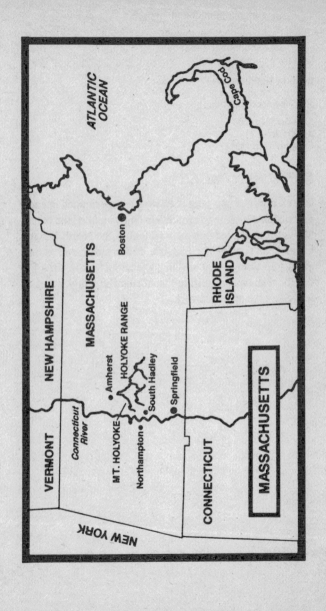

Chapter One

Connor Ryan felt a twinge of something that reminded him of stage fright. The windshield of the car
framed a house in the October twilight. It was one of
those big, old New England homes, looming amid the
sycamore trees like a proper Puritan with its sternly
whitewashed face. Connor filled his cheeks with a
mouthful of air, which he released in a reluctant sigh as
he stretched his long legs over the low-slung edge of the
rental car's door frame and planted his western boots in
the gravel driveway. The thunk of his car door settled
it. He was here now, and he'd finish this. Absently fin-
gering his breast pocket, where the hard outline of a
photograph recalled the images of a woman and a child,
he told himself he'd see it through for Kevin's sake.

It was the photograph that had brought him here, not the letter that came with it. He'd gotten at least a hundred letters from people who made every claim and declaration imaginable. Nor was it the face of the blond child, a face that certainly resembled his own. No, it was the woman's face—a perfect, porcelain oval that could have graced a hundred-year-old canvas. He could have had the letter checked out without coming here. He could have made whatever arrangements seemed appropriate. He could certainly do without kids. But he wanted to see *that* face in the flesh.

The front window brightened with lamplight and the face appeared. He'd already mounted the steps, and he knew she couldn't see him. She peered past the filmy curtains and spotted the car as he rattled the brass door knocker. The door swung open, and they stood face-to-face in the half light of evening.

"You must be Sarah Benedict."

At the sound of his voice, she took a step back, astonished. He stepped up and crossed the threshold, putting him almost a head above her. She took another step back, and she let the doorknob pass from her hand. He almost enjoyed the shock in her widening dark eyes. It was well-done. He could almost believe she thought he was a ghost. And her frosty New England coloring almost had him believing he was looking at one.

With her next step Sarah backed into the newel post. "Oh, my," she managed in a small voice. This face seemed a bit harsher, certainly more deeply tanned, and the straw-colored hair was longer, more stylish, but the resemblance was astounding. She shook her head slowly, trying to make some sense of what she saw. "You look just like... *remarkably* like..."

Connor felt a stab of pity even as he reminded himself that this beautiful lady was out to get him with the innocent-eyed shock treatment. "Kevin Ryan," he supplied. "Yes, I know. But I'm not a ghost. My name is Connor Ryan. Kevin was my brother."

Sarah stared at the proffered hand, which had never touched her but could easily have been the one that had. She watched her own hand disappear into his and found it to be smooth and warm inside. "Brother?" Allowing herself another look at his face, she told herself to stop talking like a half-wit. "Yes, I remember Kevin saying he had a brother. I don't remember mention of a *twin* brother. You must be... must have been..."

"No, we weren't twins." Her eyes were brown, he noted, and her mouth was a classic bow. Her hair was ranch mink, its shiny length reaching past her shoulders. He realized, when her hand slipped out of his, that he'd held it longer than necessary. Suddenly self-conscious, he stuffed his hands in the pockets of his jeans. "Kevin was a year younger," he explained quickly. "We were often mistaken for each other, though, after we got to be about the same size. I guess we looked a lot alike."

"Yes, you do," Sarah breathed.

"I'm sorry. I should have called first. I came... sort of on the spur of the moment."

"How did you know about me?"

He quirked her half a smile. She was good at this. "From your letter. Or your *brother's* letter."

"Jerry wrote to you? He..." Understanding dawned slowly, and embarrassment followed hard upon it. "You're the singer, aren't you? Kevin said his brother was a singer."

"Musician is what they put on my tax returns."

"And Jerry thought you might be part of a rather famous band."

"The group is pretty well-known, yes."

"He didn't... Jerry didn't..." Her distress imposed itself on her tongue, and she couldn't form the words. "I hope he didn't give you the idea that I..."

Connor glanced in the direction of the living room. "Look, maybe if you invited me in, this would be easier."

"Of course. Please..." Sarah took his soft suede jacket and hung it on the coat tree near the door. She paused while he thought to retrieve a pack of cigarettes from the jacket and watched him shove them in a shirt pocket. Then she led him into the living room, where the overstuffed furniture was all slipcovered. The room was done in blue and white, with splashes of rose. None of the tables matched, and they were all different shades of old. There was a fire in the well-used brick fireplace, and the room held a feeling of warmth and comfort. Sarah indicated a chair, but he joined her on the couch. He intended to watch that incredible face at close range.

"I suppose Jerry told you about Dannie," Sarah sighed.

"He mentioned a child—a girl." Connor drew the picture from his shirt pocket. "Is this my brother's daughter?"

Sarah glanced at the picture—the one she'd had taken at Sears during its Mother's Day special. Damn that Jerry, she thought. "Yes. She's Kevin's daughter."

"Did Kevin know about her?"

Sarah shook her head.

"Why not?" His voice carried a gruff edge.

"The last time I saw him, I suspected but I wasn't sure. I wanted to be sure. Then they sent him on one of those missions. I had a feeling..." She remembered the feeling as though it were yesterday. She was in Paris, and he'd called her. He said he was at the officers' club, and she knew he'd had a few drinks. He was gearing up for something. Kevin told her he'd be gone for a while and wouldn't be able to make it down to see her this weekend. No, he didn't know when he'd be back. No, he couldn't tell her where he was going. He'd call her as soon as he could, and they'd get together then. But she had something important to tell him. No, not over the phone. Yes, it *would* have to wait, then, wouldn't it? It would have to wait forever.

"I had a feeling, too," Connor said, his voice so much like Kevin's that Sarah could have sworn she was still on the phone. "Had a feeling he was in the wrong business." He pulled another picture from his pocket, this one of a man and a woman who could have been the two sitting on the couch. "I'd seen you before," he said, handing her the picture. "He sent that to me. That is you, isn't it?"

"Yes. It was taken in Paris...that summer." She smiled at the memory.

Connor had to hold on tight to keep his heart from going out to her. She looked quite forlorn, all right—the very picture of the girl left behind, still not quite over her soldier boy's death even after all this time. "I recognized the Eiffel Tower right away. You're going to be amazed at how observant I can be, Sarah Benedict. How long did you know my brother?"

His piercing blue eyes made her uncomfortable. She remembered that Kevin's eyes had always put her at ease. "Almost a year. We met when I was teaching adult-education classes at the post in Wiesbaden. When the class ended, I went back to Paris, but we . . . we saw a lot of Europe together that summer."

"I'll bet you did. Kevin always loved traveling. You were over there teaching?" He had pulled the tip of a cigarette from the pack in his hand, and she was watching him, disapproval apparent. "Do you mind?" he asked, just before the filter end reached his mouth.

"I don't have any ashtrays," she said stiffly.

The pack hesitated, and then a forefinger pushed the chosen cigarette back in its place. "I guess that means you mind."

She saw no reason to allow him to increase the discomfort he was causing her. "I guess it does."

He stuffed the cigarette back into his pocket and leaned back, slouching into the plump cushions as he draped both arms along the back of the couch like a great-winged condor settling over a buoying current of air. As if testing its resilience, he patted the ledge of the backrest with both hands several times before attempting another conversation launch. "So what's her name?"

"Whose name?"

"The little girl. My brother's daughter."

She returned with a level gaze. "My daughter's name is Danielle. She was named for my landlady in Paris, who was very good to me after..."

"Was she born over there?" he wondered.

"No. I came home, and she was born here." She offered him a self-deprecating little smile. "The birth of my daughter marked the end of my Paris period. Being a starving artist in Paris was an adventure, but the prospect of being a starving mother with child was something else."

"Artist, huh?" Somehow he couldn't picture Kevin with an artist. "How old is Danielle?" He knew, of course. Just thought he'd confirm it.

"She's going to be five...in March."

That figured right. Almost five. "It's been five years, hasn't it?" he said, absently marveling at the number. How could it have been that long?

"Yes. Five years. Do you know...did the army tell you what happened?"

What happened. Kevin was killed; that's what happened. Kevin came back from his grand and glorious tour of duty in a regulation army casket. Connor simply shook his head, staring past Sarah into a fire that danced in the blackened brick box across the room. The body, they'd said, was charred beyond recognition.

"I never even knew where it happened," Sarah explained. "His friend Chuck told me Kevin's helicopter went down and that his body had been shipped back to his family. Of course, I had no claim on him, but I think it would have helped to...to have gone to a funeral or something."

Connor shrugged, turning his mouth down in disagreement. "Didn't help me one damned bit. I wanted to take him home, back to California, but my father insisted on Arlington, with all the military pomp and circumstance. So there we were, putting this box in the ground, and where was Kevin? He was alive last time I saw him."

He gave her a look that told her he'd never quite made his peace with it. "Somewhere in the Middle East was what they told us. Highly secret operation. We have no idea what he was doing—whether he was shot down or what. Those big choppers he flew—they can be involved in most anything, I guess."

For the first moment since he'd arrived, Sarah shared a plane of feeling with Connor. For a moment they occupied that place, the feeling of emptiness, together. "It doesn't matter how it happened, though, does it?" she noted. "He *is* dead, isn't he? That's what it comes down to."

"Yes, that's what it comes down to."

Sarah watched the fire dance in his eyes and wondered if his memories were anything like hers. Despite the physical resemblance, this man reminded her of Kevin only in incidental ways—a gesture now and then, the way his hair caught the light. Kevin had been a small-talk artist, a genius at livening things up—the kind of person everyone sought for good company. He'd had only one mood—good-natured. His brother, Connor, was obviously a man of many moods, and he hadn't made any small talk.

"Would you like to see her?" Sarah asked, gently disturbing some reverie.

"Hmm? See her?"

"Dannie. We've been out all day, and she's exhausted. She fell asleep right after supper."

"I don't want to wake her, but I would like to see her, if that's okay with you. Just to look at her, I mean." He didn't believe he'd heard himself say that. Best thing to do was find out what the woman wanted and get the hell out of here. But he was already following her upstairs to the little girl's room.

A small lamp with a wooden-pony base filled the room with soft light. Treading awkwardly across the floor on the balls of his feet, Connor felt like a gorilla in a poodle's cage. Everything in the room was pink and white and miniature. The small braided rug by the bed thankfully muffled his footsteps, and he sank his weight back onto his heels. Looking down at Dannie, her blond curls cast about her little face in disarray, he saw Kevin. The only concession her visage made to her mother was the perfect bow of a mouth. She was Kevin's daughter.

Connor wasn't thinking as he sank to one knee beside the bed. He forgot about the woman standing behind him when he reached past the glassy-eyed teddy bear and touched the fine wisps of cottony hair that framed the child's face. He caught himself smiling, and then he pulled back. He'd probably awaken her and she might start to cry or something. Swallowing convulsively, he headed for the door.

Several steps down the hallway, Connor felt more than heard Sarah at his back. He knew he should smile casually and toss off a compliment. What would Kevin have said to smooth things over? Kevin, of course, would never have gotten choked up when he wanted most to keep his cool.

"She's...she's a pretty little kid, Sarah. She looks just like Kevin."

Who looked just like you, Sarah thought. It must have been a strange moment for this man, seeing his dead brother's only child for the first time. "Do you have any children of your own?"

"Me? No. No children. I'm not married." And neither was Kevin.

Sarah paused at the top of the stairs to watch Connor hurry to the bottom, his feet passing over each step with hardly a touch of the soles. He seemed relieved to reach the floor, and he strode directly into the living room. Following, Sarah saw him go for his cigarettes again before he thought better of it. She offered him a carnival-glass dish she'd picked up at a rummage sale.

"That's not an ashtray," he noted.

"No, but it's washable." He took the dish and gratefully lit up a cigarette. "Would you like some coffee?" she asked. "I'd offer you a drink, but I don't have anything in the house."

"Figures." He blew a quick stream of smoke toward his right shoulder, away from her face. "Coffee's fine."

While she was out of the room, he busied himself with looking around. The room was homey and comfortable, but everything seemed more used than she, in her years on her own, could have made it. He wondered if the house belonged to her parents—grandparents, even—and whether they still lived here.

The paintings on the walls were the only furnishings that weren't either worn or obviously refurbished. They were originals, and they were unique in character. Connor didn't know much about art, but these looked like the kind a real art buff might like. They were certainly better than those huge things the interior decorator had put in his own living room in Santa Cruz. He took a closer look at an unframed still life of purple and white cut flowers. It had her signature in the corner.

"What do you think?"

Connor turned toward the sound of her voice, feeling almost as though he'd been caught peeping into her closet. He shrugged, smiling sheepishly. "Very nice. I don't know much about art, but I'd gladly hang these on my wall."

"That's as good a measure as any," she said. "If you enjoy seeing it every day, it's a good piece."

The tray she set on a side table bore two steaming stoneware mugs and cream and sugar. He took his coffee black, returning to the couch while she doctored hers up. Her rich brown hair, hitched back over her shoulder and draping along the side of her face as she bent toward the table, was an exotic contrast with her fair face. Below the neck it was hard to tell what she might look like. In her T-shirt and man-size flannel shirt over loose-fitting jeans, she was hardly dressed to kill. Must be her artist's outfit, Connor thought, hoping she didn't always dress like that.

"So Paris is the place to go if you want to be a starving artist," he reflected. "What do you do when you're tired of starving?"

"You come back to the land of opportunity, where you either find a job or improvise one." The opposite end of the couch offered the best view of the fire, she reasoned as she rejoined him there.

"How do you improvise a job?"

"When you have a baby to look after, you figure out what kind of employment doesn't preclude having her with you."

"And?"

"And—the obvious. Housekeeping. I have a house-keeping business."

"A housekeeping business?" He squinted at her through a lazy haze of smoke. "You mean you're a maid?"

She didn't like the sound of the word the way he said it. "I do housekeeping for a number of clients. I set my own hours, and Dannie goes with me. The pay is pretty good, and it allows me to set aside blocks of time for my painting."

"You can't make a living as an artist?" he asked. "From the looks of these, I'd say you're too good to waste your time..."

Sarah laughed, shaking her head. "After I'm dead, someone will probably realize that. But right now it isn't steady. The gallery sells a piece once in a while, but we can't depend on it. I *can* depend on people's houses getting dirty." She watched him over the rim of her cup. For some reason he appeared to be dissatisfied with that answer. Who was he to judge the worthiness of her livelihood? It was time to discuss something else. "What kind of music do you play?"

"I'm with Georgia Nights. Heard of them?" Say no and I won't be able to keep a straight face.

"I think Jerry mentioned the name of your group to me once, but it wasn't one I recognized. You're not from Georgia."

That gave him the excuse he needed to laugh. "Only when we're on tour, honey," he drawled. "Then I'm jest as down-home as suhthun fried chicken an' black-eyed peas." He enjoyed laughing with her and forgot how she'd precipitated it. "Actually, I've lived so many places, I could say I'm from anywhere. When Mike introduces me—Mike Tanner, the lead—he uses the town I've lived in that's closest to the concert city, says that's where I'm from. Works pretty slick. When I play my solo, they go crazy for the hometown boy."

"Maybe they just go crazy for your music," she suggested. Her remark seemed to surprise him, but he said nothing. "Your father was in the army, too, wasn't he? Is that why you moved around so much?"

"Yeah. I had enough moving to last me a lifetime."

"But your business must keep you on the move quite a bit."

His left hand signaled a correction. "I have to travel, maybe, but I don't have to *move*. I have a house of my own now, and it's always in the same place, always there for me to go back to. I spend a lot of time there, believe it or not. No crowds, no schedules—just me and my music."

"Is it country music your band plays?"

She certainly was working hard to convince him she didn't know who he was. He sank back into the cushions again, taking a last pull on the cigarette he'd all but forgotten and wondered why she'd decided on this ignorant tack. All it took was one look at the kid. Surely she could see she'd gotten him with that. He was good for a reasonable amount of support for Kevin's kid. What the hell?—he had the money and nothing better to do with it. And she'd already told him she was a *maid*, for God's sake. Now she was going to feed him some highbrow I'm-not-familiar-with-pop-music routine? "Country rock," he answered, crushing his cigarette into the pink dish she'd given him.

"And you sing?" she asked.

"Not usually the lead, but, yeah, I sing—play lead guitar, a little banjo, fiddle. I write some of our music."

That caught her interest. "You write music? What have you written?"

He smiled only with his mouth. Now he was cool. Now he was creative—an artist, just like her. "You remember 'Gentle On My Mind' and 'Me and Bobby McGee?'"

"Yes," she answered brightly.

"I didn't write either of those."

"Oh."

He chuckled. "I wrote 'Dressed For Dancing' and 'Your Soft Voice.'" She shook her head slowly. "How about 'Misty River Morning'?"

"Oh, yes. That's a lovely song. I've heard it. You wrote that?" He dipped his head in acknowledgment, surprised to find that her recognition of his song pleased him. "Then I have heard your music on the radio. I'm sorry—I guess I don't pay that much attention to the names of the groups, but I remember the song well."

"That song did well for us," he admitted. "What kind of music do you like? Classical?"

Sarah lifted a shoulder. "I listen to whatever suits my mood. I'm not very trendy. I guess I'm not much for real hard rock or... or the real twangy country stuff. When I hear something I like, I listen."

"Sort of like me with the painting," he observed.

"Exactly. I don't buy records, though, so I don't always take note of the... artists' names." She smiled around the word that gave them a common bond.

"Yeah, well, I bought some paintings that this decorator lady said I needed, but I like yours a whole lot better. Think I'll throw that stuff out and start over."

Throw it out! Why did money have to be wasted on the rich? "Is your group as popular as Jerry claims?"

Connor stiffened visibly. That's right, Sarah, let's see your true colors now. "We had the best-selling country album last year. We're doing pretty well."

"Funny. Kevin said you were a singer, but he didn't tell me you were..."

"I wasn't then." One of life's great unfairnesses was that Kevin hadn't lived to see Connor's success. He took his cup up from the end table and drained what was left of the lukewarm coffee. "And obviously I've yet to make an impression in... what town is this?"

"Amherst."

"I've yet to win some of the prominent hearts in Amherst, Massachusetts. Let's see if I can remedy that, shall we? What do you need, Sarah?"

"What do you mean?"

"What do you need for Dannie? And for yourself, too. Hell, Kevin owes you. Do you want a trust fund and a monthly allowance? That's probably the best way in the long run, although..."

"What are you talking about?" Sarah bit out, each word pronounced more precisely than the last.

"Listen, I'm not going to be able to fill in for Kevin, much as I'd like to." He gave her a quick but appreciative once-over. "But I can handle being a rich uncle. Kevin was my only brother. Far as I know, this is his only kid. I *would* like to be able to see her sometimes, if that's—"

"You are way out of line, *Mr.* Ryan," Sarah said quietly. If Connor had known her better, he'd have recognized her growing anger. The angrier she got, the quieter and more measured her words became. "I don't care who you are or what you do for a living. I want *none* of your money."

"What do you mean, none of my money? What do you want, then?"

"Mr. Ryan, you are the one who came to *my* home. You came to see *my* daughter, which I have allowed you to do."

"Right. And there's no doubt in my mind now—she's my niece. I'm willing to pay...."

"There's no charge, Mr. Ryan. You are, as you say, her uncle. I won't charge you for admission into her life. With my supervision, you may visit my daughter. She has precious little family, and if you want to take your place as part of that, then fine. But we neither need nor want your money."

Connor couldn't figure this one out. She really didn't sound like she was angling for anything. In fact, she sounded downright mad. He'd never had much patience with being tactful. "Listen, Sarah, I'm not saying you aren't doing fine on your own. You're obviously working pretty hard, and you deserve a break. I really don't mind helping out with Kevin's kid. Hey—'' he punctuated his innocence with an open palm and a single-shouldered shrug ''—you wouldn't believe the way people come after you with all kinds of stories. I've been threatened with more than one paternity suit. I've had letters from at least a hundred high-school girlfriends. Somebody forgot to tell me what a great adolescence I had.'' He shook his head in mock disbelief. ''I must have been a hell of a stud.''

That got a sudden burst of laughter out of her, and Connor felt the muscles in his back relax. He hadn't realized he'd tensed up that much. Laughing with her, he continued the story, hoping he was facilitating a mood change. ''I pretty much discount the ones who remember how witty and charming I was. I figure that must have been Kevin using my ID.''

He had her smiling, mainly because she imagined there were lots of Jerrys in the world, and people like Connor must have dealt with the best of them. Jerry was such a bungler, and he'd answer to Sarah for this one. ''But you don't discount all the letters, and you're willing to donate your money,'' she surmised, ''when you think someone deserves a break.''

''When the request is reasonable and the grounds are legitimate, yes.''

''And how are those conditions determined?''

''Usually my accountant determines 'reasonable' and my attorney decides 'legitimate.' But in this case...''

''And just what was my brother's request?'' she asked quietly.

"He didn't come right out and ask for anything, really. He said he knew I was coming to Springfield for a concert, and he thought I might like to meet my brother's daughter. He had all the right details and sent the right picture to pique my interest."

"I see." Maybe Jerry wasn't such a bungler after all. It sounded as though he'd researched this quite carefully.

"It's a nice picture," Connor noted, leaning slightly toward her now because she was talking so quietly.

"Dannie's very photogenic."

"It's a nice picture of you."

His eyes caught hers, and again the sharp blue gaze seemed to rivet her soul, penetrating more deeply than Kevin's ever had. He held her that way for a time, then released her at his leisure. "So nobody's asked for anything," Connor concluded, "but I'm offering anyway."

"Thank you for the offer."

"You know, you could have gotten child support from the army. Under the circumstances..."

"I know that," she assured him, reaching for his cup. "More coffee?"

"No, thanks. You wouldn't have to feel like that was charity or anything. It would be more like you were giving Kevin a chance to support his child. He was a career officer, you know. Bound to have been a thirty-year man like his father."

"I wasn't married to Kevin," Sarah reminded him patiently. "Danielle has my name."

A slight frown clouded Connor's face. "But if Kevin had lived, you would have been married."

The cups were deposited on the tray, which gave Sarah the opportunity to hide a smile. For all his contemporary fame, there was something about Connor that rang with the charm of old-world propriety. He was here to do the right thing by his brother's child because Kevin had died before he could do the right thing himself. It wouldn't surprise her if Connor proposed marriage once he was fully convinced she wasn't an opportunist, tossing his freedom to the wind to save the Ryan name.

"I don't know what would have happened if Kevin had lived." It was as honest an assessment as she'd ever been able to come up with in all her "what-if" deliberations since Kevin's death. "We were two very different people, but in that situation, living overseas, the mere fact that we were both Americans gave us common ground. Here, of course, that would have meant exactly nothing."

"You mean . . . you didn't love him?" For some reason, that possibility set uneasily in his stomach.

"Oh, yes, I loved him very much. What's not to love with Kevin?" Sarah smiled, knowing Connor would understand. "He was everybody's friend—always pleasant, always optimistic, always had a good story to tell. But he belonged to the army. We saw Europe together—Paris, Nice, Venice, Florence—the most romantic cities in the world. That part was all my romantic fantasies come true. But if I never see the inside of another officers' club, that'll be fine with me. That was one part of Kevin's life I could never have shared. I loved him, but I don't know whether I could have lived with him."

"Yet you had his baby," Connor pointed out.

Sarah heard his indignation and thought only that it was understandable under the circumstances. "Yes, I did. What do you say about the untimely birth of the child who's become the light of your life? That she was a mistake? I know now that I was very careless and that I was foolish in my relationship with Kevin. I only knew how I felt. I didn't think ahead. I had no business letting myself get pregnant."

And Kevin had no business getting you pregnant. I heard the same lectures he did. "You could have terminated it," he said flatly.

"Oh, but I thank God I didn't. I can't imagine being without Dannie. She's very much like Kevin, you know... always cheerful and friendly."

"And you can live with that?"

She detected a teasing sparkle in his eyes, and she refused to take offense, laughing instead with, "I can handle the budding stages. Her husband will have to live with the admirers when she becomes a full-blown crowd pleaser."

A click in his cheek and an engaging wink punctuated his agreement. "The crowds can be hard to take."

"I'm sure yours are more pressing than Kevin's ever were."

"I used to think more would be better." I used to think outdistancing Kevin would make it better. "I was wrong. I like to think there are people out there who enjoy my music, but crowds..." He smiled sheepishly with the admission. "I have to swallow my stomach every time I go out onstage."

"And when you get out there?"

"When I get out there, I don't see the crowd. I see a few faces in the front row."

"But you hear them."

"They approve, so I like hearing them. What about you? How do you feel when you sell a painting?"

"I feel a few dollars richer. Oh, yes," she agreed, studying her hands, suddenly noticing that they were speckled with paint and wishing she looked a little more presentable, "I want my work to be recognized, praised by the critics, exhibited in the best galleries." She glanced up, smiling. "I don't want a crowd, but I'd like to see a few faces in the front row."

He returned the conspiratory smile. "Yeah, well, wait till the old boyfriends start coming out of the woodwork." He slid to the edge of the couch and braced his palm on his knees. "So...are you going to take my money or what, Sarah Benedict?"

"No, Mr. Ryan, I am not going to take your money." This time she gave him a merry grin when she called him "Mr. Ryan."

"Then sell me a painting."

"What painting?"

"Any painting. They all look nice from up here in the front row."

"You don't need a painting," she protested.

"If you saw the junk in my living room, you'd eat those words, Sarah Benedict."

His eyes were dancing, and in this mood, as in the others, she'd seen the life in them was far more intense than his brother's had been. "Choose one, then."

"The one with the purple flowers," he said, tossing his chin back over his shoulder.

"It's yours, with my compliments."

"Compliments, hell," he roared, but he toned his voice down when she shushed him. "I said I wanted to *buy* it."

"Would you deny me the satisfaction of making my first donation to a culturally deprived living room?"

The squeak and slam of the front door cut the conversation short. "I didn't hear anyone drive up," Sarah said, puzzled.

"I hope Dannie's a sound sleeper," Connor mumbled, following Sarah's lead as she stood to investigate.

"Hey, Sister Sarah, I need a bunk for the night." The voice was Jerry's, and Jerry was drunk. "Pepper threw me out again."

"It's Jerry," Sarah offered in a low whisper. "Listen, I know you have every right to be furious with him, but please, not tonight. I'm afraid he's..."

Connor raised a hand in protest. "Hey, I'm not mad at anybody. I came of my own accord. What's a Pepper?"

Sarah stifled a laugh, letting it escape through her nose. "I should answer with a jingle, but I can't sing. Pepper's his girlfriend."

Jerry did a little fumbling at the coat tree before propping his shoulder against the archway and peering curiously at his sister's guest. Recognition dawned gradually through the fog. "Are you...is it really...Connor Ryan?"

"Mr. Ryan, this is my brother..."

"Jerry Bendict." He'd lost one syllable of his name, but the handshake was there. Curly brown hair, dark eyes, underweight, Jerry looked like a twenty-five-year-old teenager.

"Connor Ryan."

"Connor Ryan! Oh, wow." Having accomplished the handshake, Jerry managed a feat of even greater agility as he spun a full circle on one foot, catching himself at three-hundred-and-sixty-five degrees. "I can't believe it. Connor Ryan. You're the best there is, man! If I could play the guitar like you do..."

"Jerry..." Sarah warned.

"I really appreciated your letter, Jerry. We had no idea that Kevin had a—"

"I knew you'd feel that way, Connor. When I found out that you were little Dannie's uncle, I knew it was my duty to get in touch with you. 'Course, I suspected it for some time, but I checked it all out just to make sure. I tried to tell Sarah, but she doesn't know anything about music, and I knew she wouldn't go along with the idea of getting in touch, so I just...hell, man, I knew you'd wanna..."

"Jerry..." Sarah tried again.

"You did the right thing, Jerry," Connor assured him.

"See, Sarah? I did the right thing. For once I did the right thing. And here's Connor Ryan, standing right here on your very own floor, just as casual as you please." Jerry's attempt at giving Connor a friendly punch in the shoulder missed its mark as he whirled off balance, landing in Connor's arms.

Sarah was mortified. Connor laughed as he deposited Jerry in a nearby chair. "See now, Sister Sarah," Jerry spouted, wagging a finger at her. "We're sittin' pretty now. For once I did the right thing."

Afraid of what her brother would say next, Sarah turned pleading eyes on Connor. "You'd better go now. He can be such a blubberer when he's drunk."

"You sure you don't want me to help you get him to bed?"

"I don't think he'd go to bed as long as you're here. He'll just fall asleep in the chair, which is what he deserves."

"Pretty hardhearted of you, Sister Sarah." But Connor's sympathy was obviously for Sarah.

"Hey, Connor, ol' buddy, your concert is sold out, did you know that?" Jerry was trying to sit up straight in the chair with little success. "And you know, I couldn't get any tickets."

Humiliated, Sarah closed her eyes briefly, hoping Connor would close his ears to that familiar whine of Jerry's. Her hands found Connor's arm, and she urged him toward the door. "Really, I don't mean to be rude, but I wish you'd go now."

He covered her hand with the warmth of his, offering a reassuring squeeze. "I'll call you."

In a moment, he was gone. Her hand still tingling from the touch of his, Sarah turned an accusing glare on her brother.

He gave her that infuriating cockeyed grin of his. "I guess you're mad at me, huh?"

Chapter Two

Mad at him, yes, and Sarah stayed mad until Jerry packed up his hangover and crawled back to Pepper's. His flying eyebrows over his silly rolling eyes didn't get him anywhere with Sarah, so he finally gave up, the act causing him more pain than it was worth. He left the house reasonably happy. He'd met his idol, and though the previous night's scene came back to him only in snatches, he remembered shaking hands with "the Man."

Connor's call came midmorning. Over the phone his voice was an aural déjà vu, but Sarah's mind saw Connor, not Kevin, and that surprised her. If Dannie was awake, he wondered if he could see her. He'd flown in ahead of the group just for this purpose, and since the others wouldn't be in town until tomorrow for the concert, he had the day free. If Sarah had plans, he'd like her to go ahead with them and include him. Great! He'd be there in an hour.

"Mommy, look what I found in my closet. A big envelope with a string tied around it, just like a present."

Sarah hung the receiver on its hook and turned to watch her daughter drag a portfolio into the kitchen and plunk it down next to the table. "That was way back in the cubbyhole, Dannie. What were you looking for?"

"My pink-elephant pants. I wanna wear them today."

Sarah sighed, lowering herself to sit cross-legged on the floor by the portfolio, which Dannie was busy unlacing. "Those are much too small for you, sweetheart. I put them in with the giveaways."

Dannie flashed blue-eyed dismay at her mother. "Don't give my pink-elephant pants away! I can still fit in them. I wanna wear those today."

"Dannie, today of all days would not be a good one to wear clothes that look too small. You can wear your new corduroy bibs with the Tinker Bell on them."

Dannie brightened just as the long brown lace on the portfolio came undone in her hands. "My new ones? I don't have to save them anymore?"

"I think today's the day we were saving them for." Sarah smiled, cupping her daughter's cheek in a gesture that said, "You and me, babe." It was a sticky situation but one she and Dannie could help each other handle. "You're going to meet your uncle today, Dannie." Dannie's face puckered into a question. "Not Uncle Jerry—he's my brother. This man— Uncle...Uncle Connor..." It sounded so strange she decided she'd better practice it a few times before he came. "Uncle Connor is your father's brother. He's come all the way from California to meet you, and we're going to..."

"I thought we were going to climb the mountain today," Dannie groaned.

"We are. Uncle Connor's coming with us."

"Oh. Okay," she agreed, returning to the investigation of the portfolio. "Look, Mommy, pictures." Pulling her face back from the envelope, Dannie produced a handful of charcoal-and-pastel sketches, their colors long ago fixed with spray. "Did you make these, Mommy?"

Sarah took them from her hand and leafed through the stack. Until last night she hadn't thought about those Paris days in a long time. The sketches looked almost alien to her now, done, as they had been, by a wide-eyed ingenue who wanted nothing more than to steep herself in the great works of art and to mingle with the artists at Montmartre. She'd perfected her French as a sidewalk portrait painter. She was better than most, but the American tourists wanted their portraits done by "real" artists, which meant Frenchmen. She'd also learned the best defenses against the French flirt and the occasional ugly American. Kevin had called it classy slumming, but it was an education Sarah couldn't have gotten anywhere else.

"Who's that?" Dannie wondered, pointing to the smiling face in Sarah's hand.

"It really looks more like your Uncle Connor than your father." A tilted view of the portrait didn't change anything. "Isn't that funny? Frailty, thy name must be woman."

"My Uncle Connor?" Dannie mused, studying the pastel sketch.

"No, honey, this was your father. But your Uncle Connor looks very much like this."

"My father who was killed in the war?"

Dannie's upturned face still looked for a reasonable explanation of that term, one she'd substituted for "killed in the army" after she'd heard it recently in a movie. Sarah knew none of the words could make any sense to a four-year-old, and there wasn't much point in trying to alleviate any minor misconceptions yet. "Yes, your father who was killed. When you see your Uncle Connor, you'll know what your father looked like."

Dannie was quiet for another moment as she perused the picture again. Then she uncurled her legs one at a time and hopped to her feet. "I'm going to put my new pants on now," she decided, and she scampered around the corner and up the stairs.

The house looked infinitely better this morning. Maybe it was the sunlight. Or perhaps it was the red-and-yellow-leaf show, which was best performed by New England trees on just such an October day. Connor's heavily treaded running shoes greeted the gravel driveway like a rubberized track. The car door sang out the announcement of his arrival, and he leaped over three steps to the porch. With a conscious curb on his exuberance, he rapped the door knocker.

When the door swung open, the perfect porcelain face he expected at eye level wasn't there. He had to drop his expectations several feet to find his greeter. Hair a few shades lighter than his, eyes exactly his shade of azure, she squinted up at him against the morning sun and inquired quite efficiently, "Are you my Uncle Connor?"

"Yes, ma'am, I am."

"Then you can come in."

Connor closed the door behind him and hunkered down on his heels to greet this young relative at her eye level. For Connor, relatives were in short supply, and the more complicated his life became, the more he wished he had a close relation or two. This one looked pretty harmless, and her smile promised to be a bright spot in this day and maybe in more to come.

"You're my father's brother," Dannie instructed.

"That's right," Connor confirmed.

"And you look just like him."

"Right again."

"But he's dead and you're not."

Bull's-eye. Leave it to a kid to squeeze everything into a nutshell. No glib reply for that one.

"I'm glad you're not dead because that means you can climb the mountain with us. When I get tired of walking, you can carry me." Dannie surveyed his shoulders and mentally assessed the possibilities. "You think you can carry me?"

"Let's see if I can even lift you." Connor scooped her into his arms, and she rose on a child's favorite elevator. "You're a pretty big girl, but I'm a pretty strong guy," he assured her.

"You think we'll make it up the mountain?"

"How big a mountain is it?"

"Really big," Dannie emphasized, lifting a small hand above her head.

"Well, I'm *really* strong," Connor drawled back.

Both heads turned for Sarah's descent on the stairway. Connor felt his mouth go dry as he watched. The soft violet turtleneck under a thick plum pullover and matching slim-fitting jeans were a vast improvement over yesterday's artist's outfit. Her hair was pulled neatly back into a French braid exposing a little widow's peak, which he hadn't noticed before. She was an artist with makeup, too, for though he detected hints of pink gloss and blush and a touch of mascara that hadn't been there the night before, her appearance was soft and natural.

She looked up smiling, feeling his appraisal. "I see you two have found each other."

His sense of where he was came back to him. "Oh, yeah, recognized each other right off. I'm told my job is to carry little girls when they get tired, so we're trying it out. Do I pass muster, Dannie?"

Dannie eyed Connor as though he'd suddenly become a very strange bird. "Mommy made all the sandwiches with mayonnaise. You don't put mustard on chicken. Yuk!"

Laughing as he lowered her to the floor, Connor had the feeling that whatever this little girl came up with would delight him. "I have to get my jacket," she reported, spinning away like a dervish.

Sarah collected the backpack she'd already prepared, then loaded it and Dannie into the back seat of Connor's rental car and directed Connor along the winding road over "the Notch" and into South Hadley. The car was left in the parking lot of an isolated tavern chinked into the hillside, and Sarah led the way along the easy grade of the path in the woods. Dannie chattered as she darted out ahead, squealing at squirrels and stuffing the pockets of her jacket with acorns.

Connor carried the backpack and admired Sarah's brisk gait when she went on ahead in her attempt to keep up with Dannie's explorations. Sarah spun toward him, smiling happily and motioning for a quicker pace. He picked it up a little, noting that she hadn't lost a step, but he thought better of telling her that he liked the view from a few paces back.

He felt good. He felt youthful and exhilarated as he drank autumn's air like a draught of crisp, tangy beer. He'd forgotten that New England had an exclusive contract for top quality with the Maker of Autumn and no other place did it better. Nowhere else had he seen reds, yellows and oranges this vibrant. The smell of the woods' rich humus was one he hoped he could store in his nose, to be used later when he was stuck in some stuffy hotel-room party. This was a day for keeping in your memory—a Saturday-afternoon-football-game day, a joyride-in-the-country day...a walk-in-the-woods-with-two-pretty-girls day. He'd enjoy these moments many times over.

They had veered off the footpath at Dannie's insistence, and Sarah seemed to know where her daughter was headed. Connor ducked a low-hanging branch and shuffled through the accumulation of brittle brown leaves.

"Are you girls gonna try to tell me this is the *mountain* you were talking about?" he challenged in his best cowboy drawl. "This here ain't no *mountain*. Why, where I come from, we'd call this jus' a lil' blister on ol' Atlas's back."

"Leave it to you westerners to call this lovely place a 'blister,'" Sarah scolded. "This is Mount Holyoke, a princess of a mountain, fine boned and delicately featured—not like your big rugged peaks."

Dannie had found what she was looking for, and they slowed to a halt while she proceeded to rummage around in the rocks at the base of a gray shale ledge.

Connor plucked a mottled leaf from a tree and studied its veined red, yellow and green pattern. "Princess, huh?" He glanced down at Sarah's upturned face. "She's a pretty one; I'll grant you that. I can go along with princess of a hill. But if you want to play King of the Mountain, you have to go west, young lady."

"I like rugged peaks, too," Sarah said quietly, her eyes on his face.

"And I like delicate features," he returned.

Dannie's voice severed their eye contact. "I can't find any, Mommy."

Connor hunkered down beside Dannie, who squatted with her chin between her knees as only a four-year-old can manage. "What are you looking for, Princess?"

Dannie responded with a broad smile. Being a princess was special. "This is where I found a trilobite once."

"Oh, yeah?" Connor dug into the rock pile with her. "What's a trilobite?"

"It's a bug. About a million years old."

"You sure it's not a fish?" he asked, carefully examining a piece of shale.

"Well, maybe a bug fish," Dannie compromised.

"How about an arthropod?" he offered, tossing the shale and reaching for another.

"What's an arthropod?"

"It's a sort of a...bug fish," Connor agreed, extending a find in his hand. "How about this?"

"What?" Dannie peeked over the blunt tips of four large fingers. Sarah knelt to join the pair, curious.

"It's a fossil, too," Connor said.

Dannie took it, studied it and pocketed it. "It's just a fern. They're easy. I wish I could find another trilobite."

"Kevin and I used to hunt for arrowheads. I've got a whole box full." Uncurling himself and offering Sarah a hand, Connor concluded, "Kevin never had much patience with it, though. All he ever found was pottery shards."

"Kevin," Dannie echoed. "My father's name was Kevin, wasn't it?"

Connor and Sarah exchanged glances and dropped hands at the same instant, Connor wondering how often the name had been mentioned and Sarah realizing she said "your father" more often than "Kevin" and both more rarely as time went on.

"That's right, Princess. His name was Kevin," Connor affirmed. "Now, when are you going to show me the top of this so-called mountain?"

Connor was puffing when they reached the peak. Smoking had been cutting his wind lately, and it bothered him. He knew he'd have to quit before it also cut his vocal range. But he retreated to a spot with a good view and lit up a cigarette while Sarah took care of the contents of the backpack, which he hoped meant food. Chicken with mustard, even. He was hungry.

In his plaid shirt jacket and tight blue jeans, Connor looked as strong and hard as he'd sworn to Dannie he was. Sarah wondered how he moved with the rhythm of his music. Every rock singer seemed to have his own moves. She wondered if the young girls in his audiences went wild when he did his act for them. His hair caught the early-afternoon sun in white-gold snatches as the breeze ruffled it over his tanned forehead. Watching this man grind his hips against the back of an electric guitar would probably drive her wild, too.

With his heel he dug a hole in the dirt, took a last drag on the cigarette before he squatted and buried the last of it, killing the ash with a twist of his foot. Brushing his hands on his thighs, Connor looked up and caught Sarah staring at him. A slow smile spread across his face. The porcelain lady did a little sight-seeing herself now and then.

"Uncle Connor, will you take me up on the fire tower?" Dannie pleaded as though for the hundredth time. "Mommy won't let Uncle Jerry take me up because she says he's too silly. But you could take me, couldn't you, Uncle Connor?"

Connor helped himself to a second sandwich as he sized up the eighty-foot steel structure that stood in the clearing behind them.

"I don't want this, Mommy," Dannie said.

Sarah received the remnants of a sandwich and sacked them, saying, "Dannie, the tower is too tall."

"But you could take me, couldn't you, Uncle Connor?"

"Sure I could. You wanna see what's up there, Princess?"

"Oh, yes!"

"Oh, no!" her mother wailed. "It's too high."

"It's perfectly safe, Sarah. Look—there's a fence around the platform and a railing all the way up the steps. Let's all go up when we're done here."

Jerry had often tried to get her to climb the tower and she'd always refused. But for some reason she wanted Connor to think she was a good sport. He took her silence to be assent, and Dannie was beside herself until the leftover pumpkin bread was rewrapped and the apple cores were in the garbage sack.

"You go first, and I'll be right behind you with Dannie," Connor instructed, standing to one side with Dannie in one arm and his other hand on the rail.

"Oh . . . I don't think I . . ."

"Sure you can. I'll be right behind you. Just don't look down until we get to the top."

"Ohhh," she moaned quietly, but she'd made up her mind she was going to try. This fear of heights had crept up on her as she'd gotten older, and she didn't like it. When she was a kid, she could climb any tree her brother could. Gripping the railing, Sarah planted first one foot on a clanging step and then the other. She concentrated on the top and did pretty well until she let herself sneak a glimpse of her feet. Her stomach dropped right through the grillwork of the step and tumbled to the ground.

Connor heard her gasp. "Don't look down," he reminded her. "You're doing fine."

Don't look down. That's what they always say, she thought. Sarah's knees became glutinous, but she lifted her chin and resolutely pressed on. "'Atta girl," she heard him say. "Straight to the top, honey, you can do it."

Sarah headed for the middle of the platform immediately. When Connor and Dannie joined her, she grabbed his arm and stared ahead, never up, never *never* down. She wondered when her knees would go. Her stomach was long gone. Connor, meanwhile, was enchanted with the perfect horseshoe bend in the Connecticut River, with the blaze of color that burned across the valley like Moses' bush, with the...

"Sarah, are you all right?" The color had drained from her lips. Not a good sign.

"If we could just go back down now..." The voice was too small to be hers.

"Sure we can. We've seen enough, haven't we, Princess?" Dannie nodded happily. "We'll go first." Three steps toward the stairs, and Sarah froze in her tracks. Connor worked his arm loose from her grip and quickly draped it around her, pulling her against his side. She latched on to his jacket, a hand in front and one in back. "This isn't going to be easy, is it?" Connor mumbled. In the pocket of his shoulder he felt her shake her head.

"Okay," he resolved. "We do this in stages. Sarah, you're going to sit right down in the middle of this thing and stay put until I get Dannie down."

"Oh, no," she whispered. "Please don't leave me alone up here. I'll die."

"Mommy's gonna—"

"No, she's not." Tension on his left, and now tension on his right. "Sarah, you're scaring the k-i-d. Tell her you're all right."

"I'm fine, sweetheart." Not very convincing.

"Okay." Connor was repeating himself. "Now we all sit down together. Easy." Halfway down he became everybody's sole support. "Good going. It doesn't seem so bad now, does it?" He drew back and watched Sarah shake her head. She'd sprouted saucers for eyes and gone all chalky. Still not very convincing. Connor kept talking as he moved away from Sarah and started down the steps. "Keep your eyes right here, Sarah. Straight ahead. I'll disappear for just a minute, and then I'll be right back."

"Hold on to Dannie," she called out with what sounded like the last of her voice. Connor disappeared with Sarah's daughter, but his voice reached back to Sarah. She strained to hold on to it even as it faded with his footfalls down the stairs, and she took heart as it picked up in volume again.

"Holding on to Dannie. Be right back...I'll have you down on the ground in no time—standing on your feet, of course! You're gonna be just fine, honey...we're almost at the bottom...just two more steps...here we are! Hang in there, Sarah! I'm on my way up, baby, hold on...just a few more steps, honey, I'm flying...here—" he gasped "—here I am, Sarah."

Getting her to the top of the steps was difficult, but getting her to take the first step down presented real problems. They were steep-graded fire-escape steps, and negotiating them without looking down would be next to impossible. He should have realized that, but hindsight was . . . hindsight.

"We're going down the way we came up, honey—you looking up and me right behind you." She shook her head quickly. Her voice *was* gone. "Yes, we are. Listen, I know what I'm doing. I was an ironworker once." He was prying her left hand off the rail and turning her around. Always one step below her, one arm around her waist, the other hand on the rail, he guided her down, looking out for both of them.

"I'm a regular Spiderman. No kidding. Look up, baby. Keep looking up. I won't let you fall." Their feet scraped the metal grillwork with each slow step, and as they neared the bottom, her stiff tremors became spasmodic shudders. Finally, she sobbed.

He stopped for a moment and put both arms around her. "I won't let you fall, Sarah. Trust me. I'll get you down." His quiet reassurance steadied her, and when he asked, "Are you ready now?" she nodded, and they worked their way to the ground.

Connor braced his back against a steel support and pulled Sarah into his arms. She was shaking so badly she'd never know that he was, too. He felt small arms wrap themselves around his leg, and he reached down to pat Dannie's head.

When Sarah found her voice, it was to say, "Oh, Connor, I've never been so scared."

"Me, neither," he whispered, "but don't tell the k-i-d."

"I'm sorry I acted so foolish. I could have gotten us b-both—"

"Not a chance," he said quickly, cutting off the predictable last word for Dannie's sake.

"I c-couldn't help myself," she said, her words couched in a sob muffled in the front of his jacket.

"I know. I should have taken you seriously when you said you were scared. I wanted to be the one who could get you to go up there." He didn't know why, but he knew it was true.

"And I wanted to be able to go. I don't like being such a ni-ni-ninny." She lifted her head and began wiping furiously at her eyes. "I don't know why I'm acting like this. I've never *done* anything so ridiculous, never...."

"Hey," Connor said, catching her hand before she rubbed off her mascara. "It's okay. From now on, you're allowed to be scared of heights, and I'm going to punch out anybody who calls you a ninny."

She smiled and tried to laugh, her eyes glistening brown puddles. "Thanks," she managed to say.

"Besides, something good has come of all this." He settled her hand back on his chest and brushed a loose strand of hair over her temple.

"What?"

"You called me by my name." She gave him a puzzled look. Hadn't she been calling him by his name? "You hadn't called me Connor, and I was beginning to wonder if you wanted to call me something else."

"No. I'm glad you're Connor."

Connor smiled as he watched Sarah bend down to cuddle her daughter. It had taken a while, but he'd learned to be glad of that, too.

Solid ground felt better than it ever had before, and Sarah found the rocks, leaves and yellowing grass to be new wonders, situated as they were in the foundation of security. She wished a bluejay lots of luck, and she admonished Dannie not to disturb the hooded jack-in-the-pulpit in the woods. And, no, she didn't want any purple asters plucked from the meadow for her. Let everything keep its roots in the ground today.

Yes, Connor thought, she's rooted in the earth, deeply rooted—nothing shallow about his woman. Nothing about her screams or shouts. She's as quiet as these woods, plunked right here in the middle of a valley teeming with people. Dry twigs cracked under his feet, and the sound echoed in the woods' close womb.

Connor held Dannie on one arm, and it seemed natural that he held Sarah under the other as they drifted back to the car in the late afternoon.

"Is there a good place to eat around here that'll take us dressed the way we are?" Connor wondered as he buckled Dannie into the back seat.

"These are my new bibs," Dannie said proudly. "I got to wear them today because Mommy says my pink-elephant pants are too small. But my pink-elephant pants are my favorites. They have pink elephants right here—" two chubby hands indicated her knees and then trailed along her shins "—with trunks that go all the way down to here."

"Pink elephants, huh?" Connor tightened the seatbelt and patted Dannie's knee. "When I start seeing pink elephants on girls' knees, I know I've been on tour too long. How does Uncle Jerry like your pink elephants?"

"He gave them to me. He thinks they're funny. But now—" dramatic sigh "—they're too small."

"Don't worry, kid," he said, gently clipping her chin with a fist, "Uncle Connor will come up with something better."

"Uncle Connor's *time* is something better," came the rejoinder from the front seat.

Connor smiled at the brown eyes that peeked between the bucket seats. "Uncle Connor's got all night. Name a restaurant."

"We could go home," Sarah suggested.

"You girls did lunch. Supper's on me."

Connor protested against the diner that Sarah's often one-second-too-late directions led them to, but after three-quarters of an hour of "Oh…we should've turned there," he figured the silver-streak affair was at least at hand.

"Lots of college kids come here," Sarah explained, sliding into a booth upholstered in cracked vinyl.

"Looks like the joints I frequented as a starving guitar picker," he noted, retrieving the plastic-covered typed menu from a clip behind the napkin box.

"You were once a starving musician?" Sarah asked.

"Just another gaunt-gutted hopeful," he confirmed. "But I imagine it's classier starving in an artist's garret than in a cheap motel room."

"Someday we should compare notes. How did you get your big break?"

He shrugged, studying the menu. "I got lucky. I met someone who liked my style and introduced me to someone who had the right contacts."

The scene flashed right up on the screen for her. "And the original someone was...?"

Mmm-hmm, this was fun. "A very chic lady. The kind who never looks for a price tag on her clothes but always puts one on her favors."

"Ah, yes. A true patron of the arts." *Frailty, frailty. Well, just to see if he remembers*... "What was this lady's name?"

"Her name—" blue eyes flashed merrily over the menu "—was completely forgettable." He glanced down at the menu. "Just tell me what's safe on here."

"Everything's safe. How can ten-thousand college kids be wrong about anything as serious as food?"

"We like clams," Dannie offered. "They come in a bucket like chicken."

"Fried clams?"

"Steamed," Sarah clarified. "Right in the shell."

Connor's face became a dried prune. "Slithery, slimy steamed clams?" He got two enthusiastic nods. "Yech! I'll have Swiss steak and hope to God I can keep it down while I watch you eat those things."

He tried not to watch but he was teased unmercifully by both dyed-in-the-wool New England gourmets, who finally coaxed him into trying just one clam. It slid off the shell and into his mouth easily enough, but when Dannie warned, "Don't chew it too much; you'll get sand in your teeth," the blubbery stuff was relegated to a wad of napkin.

"Tastes like Boston Harbor," Connor growled, retreating to his beer.

"Exactly." Sarah slid another clam down her throat with practiced ease. Then she smiled sweetly as Connor rolled his eyes in disgust. "And the next time you open your mouth to do one of those accents of yours, you'll get your cheers from the *Hahvahd* contingent. Those clams stick in your throat."

"They have to get past my teeth first. Anyway, I already do that one, as you'll see tomorrow night." Her look of surprise prompted him to add, "You're coming, aren't you?"

"I don't have any—"

"I do." He patted his shirt pocket. "Right here. For you and Dannie and Jerry and what's-her-name. Down front."

"Oh, I don't know, Connor. Dannie's too young to..."

"It's just music, Sarah. We don't tell jokes or take any clothes off. We just play music."

"But it's so loud."

"The speakers will be above you, suspended from the ceiling. Just don't look up this time."

"And the crowd..."

"They won't bother you. You'll be sitting down front with the press and the jocks and the mayor. Very sedate company." He turned his offer over to Dannie, where he was sure he'd get better reception. "You wanna see what your Uncle Connor does for a living, don't you, Princess?" He got the nod he was angling for and returned to Sarah with an arched eyebrow. "I have a feeling your mother thinks it's akin to devil worship."

"I do not, Connor," Sarah protested. "I just don't want to damage her eardrums."

Connor reached across the table and cupped his hands over Dannie's ears. "You think I'd damage these eardrums? No way!"

"Oh, well, I guess...I do want to...and Jerry would kill me if I..."

The advantage was suddenly his. "And after the concert, Jerry pays me what he owes me by taking the k-i-d home so you can party with me. This is the end of the tour."

"Oh, no, Connor, I don't know those people, and I wouldn't..."

"I'm the only one you need to know. The rest are just window dressing," he proclaimed, suddenly feeling so good he knew it had to be the truth.

It was so quiet on the way home Connor thought both of his girls were asleep. *His girls.* Well, okay, maybe he was presuming too much. Dannie was Sarah's, and Sarah had been Kevin's and Connor had never been much inclined to be *anybody's.* So the thought might be a hell of a bad notion. On the other hand, right now, parked here in her driveway with that soft face so close by, everything felt just right.

Carrying Dannie up to her room felt right to Connor, too. For Sarah the sight of her little girl being carried up the stairs by a man who showed every sign of caring for her was an unexpected balm for an ache she'd felt so long she'd simply allowed herself to adjust to its constancy. She'd always resented that pain, and now maybe she resented the balm a little, too. But if this man had love to give Dannie, Sarah was determined not to begrudge either of them.

Sarah made coffee, and without asking permission Connor got a fire going in the fireplace. He didn't feel that he had to check with her, and Sarah smiled her approval when she brought the coffee and saw the blaze. He sat next to her on the couch, closer this time than he had the night before.

He took the coffee and thought about a cigarette. He wasn't planning on one, just thinking about one, and what he thought was that he didn't need one. He tilted his head to look at the back of Sarah's head and the intricate braid that marked its midpoint. His hands wanted to be busy with other things. Sipping the hot coffee, he caught her eyes with his, and his smile drew a tentative little one from that bow of a mouth. His mouth wanted to be busy with other things, too.

Sarah felt a surging tingle inside her skin, and it made her uneasy. She wanted simply to be quiet and comfortable with this man. She wanted him to confine his pulse-rate manipulations to the teenyboppers, or whoever his fans were. They could handle that sort of thing. Sarah couldn't. Sarah was a very private person who...who was tingling, hot and cold at the same time inside her skin. He'd just slipped the elastic from her braid.

Defenses, to the front line. "Don't say something corny like, 'I've been wanting to do this all day,'" Sarah warned.

"I'm not going to say much," he promised, beginning the unbraiding near the bottom. "I just like to touch the things I admire. I'm like a kid—very tactile."

He continued to sip his coffee and to play at the process of unbraiding her hair. When he had it undone, he used his fingers as a comb, enjoying the way the zigzagging waves felt as they slipped between his fingers. He glanced at her coffee. Since she'd hardly touched it, he assumed she didn't really want it and he set both cups aside.

His hands carried her face closer to his, and he heard her draw a shaky breath. One soft kiss fell at the corner of her mouth. "I just want to kiss you, Sarah." Another teasing kiss, and then he murmured against her mouth, "And, yes, I've wanted to all day."

It began tentatively, his mouth testing hers, asking what she wanted, what she needed. Her lips responded with a tiny flutter. *I want closeness. I need gentleness.* He took that flutter, rising slowly on its promise, and gave a more tangible caress. Their lips danced briefly, taking the first lessons in an unfamiliar step. Then there was a sharp intake of breath, a soft moan and a sudden lack of patience to come to know the taste of each other. Connor's hands dived deep into her hair, and Sarah's arms reached under his to surround his back, pulling him closer. His kiss was hard and wild. His tongue sought a mate, and hers met it.

Intentionally entangled in her hair, his hands were not free to touch any other part of her. He would know her with his mouth now, and he would tease himself a little because his gambit had suggested just a kiss. *I just want to devour you, Sarah,* he thought. *I just want to be ab-*

sorbed in your softness while you take all the world's hardness away.

Sarah lifted her chin to welcome the sweet wet touchings on her neck. If she voiced the welcome that rang in her ears as it coursed throughout her veins, she knew it would be all over but the recriminations. But how good it was to feel this much life in her every nerve. How sweet to have someone to cling to, however briefly. Connor, hold me closer. Connor, touch me. Connor, don't let me give this a second thought because if I do...

"Connor, this could lead to real...complications."

He nudged a kiss into her ear. Complications. A euphemism for involvement without commitment. Who could blame her for fearing that kind of thing? "I'm just kissing you, Sarah. Kisses aren't complicated."

"Yours are," she groaned.

"No, they're not," he protested, nuzzling the sleek hair at her temple. "Very simple. Just you and me and our kisses tonight."

"Your kisses are very...sticky." She let her hands slide down the cool cotton of his shirt and rest at his sides.

He chuckled softly near her ear. "Dannie's are sticky, honey. Mine are just a little wet."

"Dangerous when wet."

He drew back, smiling as he untangled his fingers and smoothed back her hair. "Slid right into my arms, didn't you?"

"I'm afraid I—"

"Don't be." He touched her cheek and shook his head. "Don't be. I know you haven't got it straight in your head who I am yet. There are lots of things I've wanted to do all day, Sarah Benedict, but I'll wait until you know, until you're sure."

"Too many people know who you are, Connor. That scares me." He put his arm around her and cuddled her against him, and that didn't scare her.

"Not as many as you think. When you're part of a group, you can usually walk down the street just like anybody else—unless you're in town for a concert. People are kind of looking for you then."

"You do pick high-profile jobs, Connor Ryan. If you'd stayed an ironworker you could've taken that literally."

"Ironworker?"

She leaned back for a look at his face. "You told me you'd been an ironworker." He grinned. "You mean you weren't?"

"I've been a lot of things, honey, but I've never been *that* crazy."

Chapter Three

Sarah was faced with what she knew psychologists called an approach-avoidance conflict. She paced. She brooded. She ransacked her closet and all her drawers. Then she brooded some more. Sarah wanted to go to the concert, but she had nothing to wear. She wanted to see Connor perform, but she didn't want to watch from a front-row seat. She'd prefer some isolated little projectionist's booth or a box in a private opera house, like the sumptuous one she'd seen when she toured Versailles. *Really, Sarah. Country rock at Versailles.*

Admittedly, knowing Connor had been very nice so far. He was a very attractive man with a warm personality and a fine sense of humor. But then there was also this vague notion that elsewhere he'd be something larger than life, a fantasy that everyone wanted a piece of. Here in her house he was simply a man, and that was complicated enough.

In the back of her closet she found a skirt she hadn't worn in a long time. A leather-craftsman friend of hers had made it in trade for a painting. Sarah had a number of handmade treasures she'd acquired that way. The skirt was butternut kidskin, and she could wear it with the matching boots she'd bought in Italy and her pale yellow Italian silk blouse.

Dannie wasn't sure what all the excitement was about, but she knew that her new uncle was somehow involved, and he'd already assumed hero status with his little niece. She thought he'd like her blue calico smock with the white pinafore because it was a pretty dress, and princesses wore pretty dresses. She scolded Uncle Jerry for not dressing up, but he told her that T-shirts and blue jeans were all he had.

"That's all the roadies ever wear," Jerry protested.

Sarah withdrew her all-weather coat from the front closet near the stairs, only half-interested in an answer when she asked, "Roadies?"

"Roadies are people who travel with the group to take care of equipment, sell souvenirs, run errands, that sort of thing," Jerry explained. "Wouldn't I make a great roadie?"

Sarah's eyes narrowed. "Jerry, if you even hint at asking for favors from that man again, I will never forgive you. You've caused enough..."

"What have I caused?" The arm he draped over his sister's shoulders wasn't intended to be patronizing. "I've gotten some people together. What's the harm in that? The man deserved to know about his dead brother's daughter.''

She's *my* daughter, Sarah's brain screamed, but Dannie was sitting at the bottom of the steps buckling a shoe, and she couldn't be expected to understand why Sarah took exception to all this sudden talk of *Kevin's* daughter. ''All right, now you've told him. But I don't want him to think we want anything from him. Not *anything*, Jerry.''

Jerry smiled his sweet, crooked smile. ''I won't ask for anything. But wouldn't it be fun to travel with a band like that, Sarah? Wouldn't it be a great life?''

With a motherly, one-armed squeeze, Sarah drew back to put her coat on. Jerry lifted a hand in one of his typically ineffectual overtures of assistance, managing, as always, to be just a little late. Lifting her hair at the back to free it from her coat, Sarah clucked an indulgent ''tsk'' at Jerry, adding, ''At twenty-five you're still trying to decide what you want to be when you grow up.''

Jerry laughed. ''I know what I want to be. I want to be rich and famous. I just haven't figured all the angles yet.''

There was no point in commenting. Jerry would go to his grave believing there were easy angles he'd missed out on. ''Are we picking Pepper up on the way?''

''Pepper's not coming,'' Jerry said, a twinge of guilt nudging his chin toward his chest.

''Why not? I gave you her ticket.''

''I know. I scalped it.''

''You...Jerry, you have absolutely no...no conscience,'' Sarah stammered.

"Hey, she kicked me out the other night, Sarah. I had to hitch a ride over here. I don't like going back with my tail tucked between my legs every time I get a little buzzed. I don't need that, Sarah."

"Maybe not." Taking Dannie by the hand, she headed for the door, tossing back, "But you do need a place to stay, don't you, Jerry?"

The truth struck Jerry as funny. "Yeah, I do. And if you don't want me back here, don't say anything to Pepper about that ticket."

From behind the stage, Connor witnessed their arrival. Sarah was a classical beauty, simply stated. He'd seen too many groupies in their blue jeans—blue jeans with T-shirts, blue jeans with fancy blouses, but always the blue jeans. He tucked his thumbs into his western belt behind his back. Blue jeans for him, too. It was part of the image—comfortable, casual, one of the folks.

Smiling in Sarah's direction, though there was no possibility that she could see him, he turned her name over in his mind a few times. She wasn't a groupie; she wasn't even a fan. She was here as a friend, just to see him. That bit of consideration was what he'd wanted from his parents, what he would've had from Kevin if things had been different. But that was water under the bridge, and this was someone else. This was Sarah.

He watched her sit down, fuss over Dannie's hair a little bit and then respond to something Dannie pointed to in the program book. Unless she had him totally buffaloed with the fierce independence she professed, Sarah wasn't interested in images. She was here just to see him. He'd show her how good he was at what he did. She'd like his music because he knew how to make great music, and tonight he'd make it even better than great.

"What's out there, Connor?" The hand on his shoulder belonged to Scotch Hagan, the big, red-headed, bushy-bearded drummer for Georgia Nights. "See any pretty faces in the front row?"

"One," said Connor, and then he amended. "Two, but the second one's wearing ruffles and ankle socks."

"What's the first one wearing?"

Sarah turned wide eyes over her shoulder as one boisterous fan hooted a greeting at another behind her. Connor chuckled. "A nervous smile."

The house lights went down and then out, and the crowd quieted, waiting, watching the dark stage. Movement on stage brought forth a low buzzing from the audience, one anticipatory "Yeah!" from the bleachers, then a high-pitched "Whoa!" from the opposite side. At once the stage was flooded with white light and the imperative of a rock-hard downbeat. Cheers from the audience melded with the music, and the electrical connection was instantly complete. Four microphones, four voices, four instruments, one sound—one complete circuit with the audience.

The intro was a pacemaker for those whose hearts beat in four-four time. The lead singer's rhythm guitar tagged into the drummer's beat while Connor's guitar laid down a track for the lusty male voices to ride on. Head tilted back in amazement, Sarah watched Connor's hands wrench the hard-driving melody from the taut strings, heard him belt out the demands in the chorus, saw him lean over the neck of the instrument and squeeze roller-coaster sounds out of the bottom end. She tried to remember the man who'd knelt by Dannie's bed and tentatively touched her hair. There was nothing tentative about those fingers now.

The first songs pitched the crowd forward in their seats and kept them speeding over the hills and around the curves of each tune. Then came the introductions, handled by the lead singer, who introduced himself as Mike Tanner from Waycross, Georgia. That drew an enthusiastic response. Then there were the jokes about Scotch Hagan's red beard and bassist Kenny Rasmussen's low voice, and then...

"The three of us, we're all from south of the Mason-Dixon line, but we got this here Yankee—" a few stray cheers "—in our midst. Ol' Connor, he's kind of a wandering minstrel. Plays lead guitar, banjo, fiddle, whatever else he can get his hands on." A female cat-call. "Don't ever let him get his hands on *you*, honey, lemme tell ya..." Female shrieks. Connor shuffled a little uncomfortably. "No, Connor was raised up around these parts. You know these hill folk pretty well, doncha, Connor?"

Connor waited for the laughter to settle to the floor before he leaned close to the microphone and asked, "Anybody climbed the fire tower up on top of Mount Holyoke lately?" Assent came from the applause. He looked straight at Sarah, grinning with their private joke, the message that he knew she was there. "Scary, ain't it?" Sarah felt her face grow hot, warming her smile as the crowd cheered in agreement.

"Connor Ryan writes most of our music," Mike continued. "Like this one. 'Misty River Morning.'" Applause greeted the introductory chords, and Connor assumed the role of lead singer, his voice pouring over the words of the slow song like warm golden honey. Sarah felt her chest tighten as he sang the last lines— "You and me and the river, babe, makin' misty mornin' love." The sustained last note was a plea that elicited a second's silence before thundering applause.

It was Connor Ryan's night. His double-necked guitar argued with itself like a two-headed creature, provoked by fingers that could not possibly be connected with any human hand. On a bluegrass number, his sassy bow played a fast seesaw on the fiddle, the high-pitched music whirling around the stage and tumbling out to the crowd like a spinning Cossack. Mike Tanner set his guitar aside and did a mountain jig while Scotch and Kenny clapped along with the crowd. Sarah was close enough to see Connor's sweat and feel his exhilaration. The audience was his.

He sang the lead on two more songs, attesting to the pleasure of "givin' my woman all I got" and pulling at the heartstrings with memories of "the dusty echoes of a lie, a lonely, hollow, aching sigh." All of the music was a natural extension of Connor and his instrument. Even the songs the lead singer sang seemed to be showcases for Connor in one way or another. Sarah would not remember what Mike Tanner had sung in the shadow of Connor's performance.

"Hey, you Georgia boys, I got an idea!" Mike shouted through the speakers.

"Yeah?" came three practiced replies.

"What say we . . . scare up some brew . . ."

"Yeah?" Scattered cheers.

"And some tunes . . ."

"Yeah?" Anticipation.

"And some Springfield boys and girls . . ."

"Yeah?" Whistles. "I like that last part," Scotch put in.

"And see if Springfield knows . . ."

"Knows what, Mike?" Scotch prompted amid a growing volume of yells.

"Knows how to par-ty!"

The lyrics, what were distinguishable, reveled in the prospect of "gettin' a rockin'-good party goin' tonight," and there was hand-clapping, foot-stomping pandemonium in response. Connor's euphoria was no less dramatic than the rest, and the party seemed to have started already. Sarah stood with the crowd while Jerry bounced Dannie in his arms and sang along. The foot stomping in the bleachers became deafening. Sarah felt raw panic rising in her throat. Uniformed policemen kept the crowd from swarming the stage, but Connor didn't seem to notice that there wasn't much between him and this growing madness except a few stern faces. He continued to pour total enthusiasm into the song. Sarah envisioned an army of crazed music lovers pouring from the bleachers to descend upon the band the minute this was over.

But it didn't happen. The group obliged the roaring crowd with one encore and then another, but with the dawn of the house lights, the single-voiced crowd began to break apart into individual pieces. Several thousand cars would have to be moved into the streets of

Springfield. Therefore, since no one accepts the challenge of cutting into traffic quite like the Massachusetts driver, it was every man for himself.

"Miss Benedict?" Sarah turned to find a young man in a black Georgia Nights T-shirt looking like the proud bearer of an official message. "Will you follow me, please?"

"Follow you where?"

"Right this way. You have a friend backstage." His eyes hinted at connotations suggested by the word "friend."

Sarah complied, and Jerry brought up the rear with Dannie in his arms. The young man swung him an unwelcome look, but Jerry informed him, "I'm with her."

"Yes, he is," Sarah agreed, reaching for Dannie.

Shouldering his way past fans and security guards, the young man led them down a corridor, obviously quite taken with his own privileged status. Jerry caught Sarah's attention and widely mouthed the news that this was a roadie. Sarah nodded without the enthusiasm that Jerry would have considered appropriate.

The roadie's knock brought Connor to the dressing-room door, which he swung open with a smiling flourish. "This the right lady, Connor?"

"*These* are just the *ladies* I wanted to see. Thanks, Rob." The roadie took his leave as Dannie readily transferred herself into Connor's waiting hands. "Hey, Princess, what'd you think?"

"That *was* you, Uncle Connor! You were very loud. I wish I could sing that loud."

"Loud, huh?" Connor laughed. "I don't know how to take that. Was I any good?"

"Oh, yes, very good—and wonderfully loud. Did you take a shower with your clothes on, Uncle Connor?"

"Not yet, but it sounds like a good idea. Here..." He lowered her to a padded swivel chair. "I'm getting your pretty dress all wet. Lights must've been pretty hot tonight."

Jerry was about to burst with excitement as he bounced on the balls of his feet and split his face with a grin. "That's honest, working man's sweat, Connor. You really know how to make that fiddle sing, and that double-neck... I never heard anything like it."

The compliments were nice, but they hadn't yet come from the right quarter. Connor felt Sarah's eyes on him, and he tingled with the need to hear her voice. He looked past Jerry to find her eyes ashimmer with unspoken praise.

She hung back, feeling awed, feeling shy. His plain white western shirt, sleeves rolled just below his elbows, stuck to him in opaque wetness. His hair was a shade darker damp than it was dry, and it formed more waves and curls. He looked exhausted, but the excitement lingered in his eyes.

"Did you like the concert, Sarah?"

She stepped closer, ignoring Jerry's presence, hardly noting Dannie's. She saw that her answer was important to him. "The concert was a little overwhelming, Connor. But you... you were *completely* overwhelming. I became... totally absorbed in your music."

"Are you tempted to buy a record?" he wondered, and she nodded, smiling. "Terrific! If we've made a fan of Sarah Benedict, we must have the rest of these pilgrims in the palms of our hands. I'll see that you get autographed copies of all the albums," he promised. "And something decent to play them on."

"Oh, no... actually, I think we'll get a stereo soon— maybe for Christmas this year."

"I think so, too." He turned a winning smile on Dannie. "Did you know Santa has a reindeer named Connor, Princess?" Dannie matched his smile and shook her head. "Sure. Comet, Cupid, Connor and Blitzen. Big, strapping brute. They use him to pull the sleigh when it's full of stereo equipment."

"I want a dollhouse for Christmas," Dannie announced.

"He's the one who brings the dollhouses, too." Connor gave her a chuck under the chin. "So you leave him some oatmeal cookies, okay? He likes oatmeal cookies."

"Connor..."

He cocked an eyebrow at Sarah along with gift-giver's eyes. "Oatmeal cookies," he emphasized. "With lots of raisins." Turning to Jerry, he laid the charm in double layers. "Listen, buddy, I really appreciate your staying with Dannie for a while so I can have a date with her mother. We won't be too late. I promise."

"Bet that's gonna be some party," Jerry said, his voice convincingly wistful. "Sarah's never been much for parties. Don't know how she got related to me."

"Well, I'm not much for parties, either," Connor said, "but these are my friends, and I want them to meet Sarah." Connor's hand on his shoulder pumped Jerry up to double his size, and the "Thanks, man, I knew I could count on you" was the clincher.

A limousine sped Sarah, Connor and Scotch Hagan to the hotel in dark-windowed anonymity. Such luxury made Sarah uneasy, and she couldn't bring herself to let her back relax against the plush upholstery. She assured Scotch that she'd enjoyed the concert and expressed appropriate appreciation for his compliments on her beauty, which struck her as so much Southern charm. Clutching her purse in her lap, she watched the familiar streets pass by the car window with dread anticipation of what was to come.

"Sarah's an artist," Connor told Scotch. "You should see her paintings. Really fine work. I've been trying to get her to sell me one, but she doesn't believe I'm a real connoisseur."

"He's not," Scotch said with a nod in Sarah's direction. "I gave him a hand-thrown pot once, and you know what he did with it? He filled it with horse feed."

"What else do you do with a pot that size?"

Sarah understood immediately. "Are you a potter, Scotch?"

Shrugging a bit sheepishly, Scotch nodded. "I kind of putter, I guess. I have a wheel and a kiln. I like to mess around in the clay."

"You mean you made that?" Connor asked, amazed. "You never told me...."

"Not after you filled it full of horse feed, I wasn't gonna tell you." Scotch glowered for a moment and then burst out laughing. "Some connoisseur. If you can't play it on the guitar, our boy here don't know nothing about it. Unless it's a pretty girl. And then ol' Connor sure can pick 'em." Sarah was treated to a red-lashed wink.

Connor took Sarah to his suite, where she listened to the radio while he showered and changed. The pop-music station was featuring Georgia Nights in honor of their visit to Springfield. She remembered the way Connor's body moved with the music, the slight roll of his hips and the occasionally emphatic swing and sway of his shoulders as he pounded out the climax of a song. She'd never be able to listen to this music without remembering the sheen on his forehead and the bright excitement in his eyes, an excitement that translated into wattage in Sarah's own bloodstream even now.

Connor burst from the bedroom on the tail end of the hurry he'd been in to avoid keeping her waiting. Sarah interpreted it as a rush to get to the party, and she sat up straight in her chair, her spine stiffening.

"Did I tell you how great you look tonight?" he wondered. "That skirt is terrific."

"Thank you," she murmured, brushing at the spotless leather. "A friend made it. You . . . um . . . you look very nice, too."

Laughing off the sudden awkwardness, Connor reached for her hand and drew her to her feet. "Nice" was an understatement, and she wondered whether he knew it. He seemed totally unconscious of his looks, unaware of the fact that everything he wore seemed to accommodate itself perfectly to his frame. His pearl-gray pullover with stylish satin insets at the shoulders and open-flap neckline flattered his broad shoulders and long torso. Gray jeans and boots hardly gave him a California look, but then he was hardly Californian—or maybe he was truly Californian. He was the man from all over America.

"Connor, I know most people, including my impossible brother, would give their eyeteeth to go to this party, but I'm afraid I'm going to be such a dud. I just don't do well at parties."

"You don't have to do anything, Sarah. Just make it very obvious that you're with me, and we'll both be fine."

Sarah found that to be a taller order than it had sounded. The party was already under way in a large suite. The private bar was open, and it was apparent that they'd certainly managed to scare up some Springfield girls. Sarah was introduced to Mike Tanner, with his dark hair that hung to his shoulders and a neatly trimmed beard. His woolly chest completed the hairy look, since he'd not found time to button his shirt. Mike seemed more than pleased to meet Sarah, as did Kenny Rasmussen, whose low-pitched Southern drawl was a startling contrast with his fair-haired, boyish appearance.

Besides Connor, Sarah quickly decided she liked Scotch the best. Everyone else seemed too quick with a laugh. Mike asked her where she was from and gave a high sign over her head to someone behind her just as she opened her mouth with an answer. Over her head he proceeded to effect a bushy raised brow, a wounded frown and a mimed denial before recovering his end of the conversation.

"Whereabouts did you say, hon?" A slurp of beer drew his interest next.

"I didn't."

"Ahh, mystery lady. I like that. This one's cool, Connor. Real New England-style cool." Even as he gave

Connor a friendly slap on the back, Mike's eye was scanning the crowd. "See if I can find me one just like her."

"I wish you luck, my friend," Connor offered, shaking his head after the man.

"He's already outta luck." The hand on Sarah's shoulder gave her a start, but she relaxed somewhat when she caught Scotch's smile. He'd hooked his other wrist over Connor's shoulder. "Not a one like our Sarah. I already checked."

"*Our* Sarah? I never heard you say *our* Maggie," Connor said.

"I let her feed you once a month, though," Scotch reminded him, turning to Sarah with the explanation, "This is Connor's way of letting you know that I'm the only one of the bunch who's respectfully married and perfectly harmless."

Connor gave Scotch's beard a playful tug. "Faithful as an ol' red setter."

"Gotta be. You oughta see my ol' lady. Big as a Louisiana bayou and twice as snaky. Her daddy was an alligator, and she's got the teeth to prove it." He was gratified by Sarah's small laughter. Scotch knew the poor girl was terrified of this whole scene—anybody could see that. Maggie had never warmed up to it, either. "This boy's got no manners, Sarah. Lord knows we've tried to teach him the meaning of Southern hospitality, but he just can't seem to get it down. What can I get you to drink?"

"I'm just fine, really."

"I'll bet you'd like a little white wine or maybe a spritzer?"

"Yes, actually I think I would."

Scotch moved toward the bar like a gentleman with a mission, never sidetracked. "I'd have offered first," Connor said, "but Scotch likes to play host. Keeps him busy."

"And I'll bet his wife isn't big or mean or snaky," Sarah guessed.

The light in Connor's eyes told Sarah that Maggie was special to him, too. He shook his head, smiling. "Maggie's a gem. He'd have hell to pay if she heard him call her his 'ol' lady.' They have two redheaded rascals, one Dannie's age. And they have..." Sarah caught a wistful look, a quick wish. "They have a nice home in Nashville."

"And you visit them once a month?"

"We record in Nashville, and I have an apartment there. When I'm in town, Maggie puts the welcome mat out." Scotch was back with a beer for Connor and Sarah's glass of wine. "Thank you, my man," Connor said with a nod, repeating, "She's a gem, that wife of yours, Scotch."

"That she is," Scotch agreed. "And our Sarah's a lady, Connor. You don't wanna keep her hangin' around this party too long. I have a feeling we'll be paying for damages again."

Connor scanned the room and nodded in agreement, but the idea seemed to amuse him. Sarah didn't think it was a funny prospect at all.

Guests included roadies, technicians, local disc jockeys, people who knew the right people, and the right people themselves, whose sphere of influence was not always altogether clear. Among them were several attractive women who were obviously aware that they were there simply by that virtue.

One persistent brunette tried to strike up a conversation with Connor, offering Sarah a plastic smile and a perfunctory nod before putting her wit on the line with, "You were wonderful tonight, Connor. I felt your energy pouring directly into my body and I thought, 'A Leo. He has to be.' I'm totally compatible with Leos, and I know one the minute I see one. Can you guess what sign I was born under?"

Deadpan expression, absolute innocence. "The sign of the spider. That's one, isn't it?"

"If you want it to be," she tried.

Connor leaned closer, and her eyes fluttered to half-mast before the promise of his slow smile. "Go try Mike, then. I think he was born under the sign of the fly." Her eyes followed the direction of Connor's nod.

The interest in Connor wasn't all as obviously sexual, but most of it seemed no less opportunistic. The right people were interested in him nowadays because he was money. Sarah was introduced to a woman named Sally, who seemed to be in charge of seeing that Connor and the other members of the band greeted the people who expected to be greeted. Connor smiled and nodded and answered most of their questions, appreciated their praise. Sarah remembered the way Kevin had enjoyed this kind of scene. But while Connor was pleasant, he wasn't glib, and he kept Sarah close to him. She wondered if he could be as uncomfortable as she was.

Sarah became increasingly awkward as the sea of eyes around her got glassier and the grins became loose and rubbery. She didn't want to think about what might be responsible for those fish-eyed looks.

"Ready to go?" Connor's face was blessedly sober. Sarah answered with a grateful nod.

"Hey, Connor, come on over here and pick some with us."

Connor's face clouded slightly as he sighed. Mike needed Connor to make him look good. This was the point at every party where Mike plugged his hose into Connor's guitar and depended on Connor to inflate him. Mike had a good voice, but he hadn't grown with his success. It was getting harder to keep Mike sober before a performance and harder still to tolerate him afterward.

"Come on, boy, we need those magic fingers. Sheila here needs a little orientation in country music." Mike saw Connor's reluctance, and he wasn't above a little subtle pleading. "Come on over; we'll give her the short course. Ten minutes."

Ten minutes. He could give Mike that. Ten minutes would buy Mike a whole night of the kind of fawning he enjoyed. Connor checked his watch. Still pretty early by Georgia time. "Ten minutes," he agreed.

Sarah's heart slid down a mental rain gutter. She'd seen what the music did to Connor. In ten minutes he'd just be getting warmed up.

In twenty, he was hot. Where earlier there'd been genuine friendship apparent only between Connor and Scotch, now with the music the camaraderie among the four was tangible. They used folk guitars now, and Scotch tapped out a beat on a practice pad. Seated in a loose circle on a couple of stools and folding chairs,

they swung together from rhythm and blues to rocka-
billy, Connor carrying Mike like a broad-shouldered
brother. The essence of the relationship was couched in
the scene.

But for Sarah, there was more than the music. There
was the distance between herself and the man who'd
brought her here. And she felt out of place among the
sweaty, seamy, suffocating party crowd. As the bodies
pressed toward the music, she drifted back near the bar.
The faces around her became leering, distorted, inhu-
man. They were like the faces in a fun-house mirror.
This was surrealism for Sarah at its most gruesome. It
was time to call a cab.

"He's incredible, isn't he?"

The brunette had crept to her side without Sarah's
notice, and she was in the process of draping all eight of
her long, lean appendages over the bar stool next to
where Sarah stood. She splashed a shot of vodka in a
hotel glass and lifted the glass in Sarah's direction.
"May he turn out to be as good as he looks," she said,
her long, wine-colored nails coddling the glass. She read
the look in Sarah's face and thought better of downing
the shot. "You aren't staying with him tonight, are
you?"

Sarah said nothing. If real spiders could smile the way
this one did, flies would get nervous.

"You aren't a pickup." Confidently lowering the
webs in front of her eyes, the spider lady tapped her
glass with a red nail. "He's going to take you home.
And I'll be here when he gets back. A man like that has
different women for different reasons, doesn't he?"

Sarah had nothing to say. She would defy the webs.

"You're very pretty and very sweet. I'd say you've served your function, wouldn't you?"

Sarah didn't feel the vodka dribble down the front of her skirt or drip on her boot. She looked down when she smelled it. Horrified, she watched the soft butternut leather turn yellow-brown. Her dignity never faltered, but she felt like a wilting sapling. She turned a wordless glare at the creature who was responsible, refusing to acknowledge the existence of such a low form of life with a verbal condemnation. Sarah simply turned from the absurdity of the scene and walked away.

She did not take the time to mop herself up or to announce her departure. She found her coat on a rack, put it on and left the party. At the front desk she called a cab. The expense would destroy her budget, but she had gotten herself into this, and she had to get out. At this time of night, there was no other way.

The cost of the cab nearly destroyed more than Sarah's budget. The cash she had stashed in the freezer for emergencies had been "borrowed" again. She had less than half the fare in hand, and the cabbie refused to accept a check.

"Listen, lady, nobody takes a cab from Springfield to Amherst unless she's loaded one way or another. I should've guessed what kind of loaded you were. You smell like you fell into the punch bowl."

"I'm not loaded—" Sarah spat disgustedly "—either way. I wouldn't have called you unless I had the money. At least, I thought I had the money. You will be paid."

"When?"

A pair of brazen headlights swung into the driveway. Sarah squinted as they swept past her face, and the arriving car took a berth on the opposite side of the cab. The engine was abruptly shut off, and the car door was slammed. "You all right, Sarah?"

The voice struck a mellow chord, a welcome sound in the night. "Yes, I'm all right."

In the dark, his face was a twice-familiar one that caused her a quick catch of breath each time she saw it. It was no longer a face for public consumption but one reflecting private concern. He couldn't imagine what had possessed Sarah to take a cab home.

"Sarah, you should have said something. What are you doing? Did something..."

"She's telling me she doesn't have enough cash to pay her fare, that's what she's doing," came the grumble from inside the cab.

Without a word, Connor pulled out his wallet and handed some bills through the open window. "Thank you for waiting. This should make it worth your while."

"Yeah." Grinning up at Connor, the cabbie pocketed the money. "Glad somebody around here's loaded. G'night, folks."

They stood together in near darkness listening to the cab's retreat into the night, making certain of the silence, and comfortable in the knowledge that neither could see the depth of feeling in the other's eyes. It had been a near miss. He almost hadn't come, not knowing why she'd left. He'd almost indulged himself in an angry assumption. She'd almost let him go without a word of explanation. They might have let it end right there. But now he'd found her, and each one rejoiced privately.

"I wanted to take you home myself," he said quietly. "You should have told me you were..."

"I did."

"But *I* suggested we leave. You agreed, but I didn't realize it was this urgent."

"Connor, I told you I was no good at parties. You weren't ready to go. It wasn't necessary that you..."

"It was necessary," he insisted, catching her shoulders in his hands. "I got carried away and left you to fend for yourself among the—"

"I've been fending for myself quite well for some time now," Sarah informed him on a soft note of indignation. "I knew the way home, and if Jerry hadn't raided the freezer, I'd have paid for my own ride. As it is, I intend to pay you back, but I'm not responsible for your flashy tipping."

Connor took that as a sign that she wasn't completely opposed to his help or overly angry about his negligence. He dropped an arm over her shoulder, and they walked toward the front door. "No, but you're at least partly responsible for my headache, so you can pay me back in aspirin, and a little coffee on the side. And maybe we could talk awhile."

"Talk? I wonder how you can have any voice left at this point."

They'd reached the front door, and Connor took the keys from her hand. "This the right one?" It proved to be. "I get keyed up for a performance, and it takes me a while to come down. I'll talk until you fall asleep, and then I'll slip quietly away. I want to know all about Jerry and the freezer and whether you do windows and why you left without telling me."

"How about if I fix you some breakfast?" she whispered, hooking her coat on the coat tree alongside his jacket.

"Love it. Just don't forget the side order of aspirin."

Sarah shed some light on her brown-and-yellow country kitchen and took a bottle of aspirin down from the cabinet. "I hope you came by this headache honestly," she said, handing him a tall glass of water. "I'd say most of your glassy-eyed guests are in for some headaches when they come down, too. Is that all...par for the show-business course?" Her eyes phrased the question more personally.

"I had a couple of beers, which is par for *my* course," he told her. "The rest doesn't interest me. I don't need any more brain damage." The question in her eyes was rephrased. "Forget I said that." He shrugged quickly. "Poor joke. What're we having, now? I do terrific omelets. Got any mushrooms?" He rubbed his hands together briskly, dismissing the "poor joke" with serious cooking talk.

Connor allowed no interference with his omelet, so Sarah busied herself with coffee and a fruit compote. When all was ready, she hung her apron on its hook, and he noticed the front of her skirt.

"What happened there?"

Having forgotten about the stain, she wished she hadn't uncovered it now. "Spider Woman got a little clumsy," she answered lightly.

Connor remembered that about the time he'd realized Sarah was gone, the Spider had staged a second come-on, more direct than the first. He'd felt as though he'd walked into a room full of cobwebs, and he couldn't find the door fast enough.

"Is it ruined?" he asked.

"I think so." She joined him at the table.

"Damn, I liked that skirt. I'll buy you another one."

Sarah's frown lacked patience. "You can't buy another skirt like this, Connor. It was made for me by a friend. There *isn't* another skirt like this."

His shrug said otherwise. "I'll have another one made. What do you think?"

She sighed, rolling hot cheese, mushroom and eggs over her tongue. "I don't think you understand."

"I know *you* don't understand. What do you think of the omelet?"

"It's delicious. And I am not going to become your special charity. The skirt is not replaceable, and it wasn't your fault anyway, so don't worry about it."

"Of course it was my fault. It was my party. Is that why you left?"

"Yes...no, not entirely. But sometimes it takes a cold splash to bring me to my senses."

He didn't ask what her senses had told her about him after she recovered them. She was afraid of him; he knew that. He'd have to cure her of that. He found her shyness to be lovely and painful at the same time— lovely because it was so honest, and painful because he felt it, too. As long as he was making music, he didn't care if there were five or five thousand people around, but just hanging out and rubbing elbows in a crowded room was something else. He'd never quite overcome the fear of suffocating while everyone else in the crowd took all the air. He never knew when the conversation would turn to him and he'd draw an absolute blank. Most of his party appearances were brief—arrive late, meet the people, play a few tunes with the boys, exit quietly.

They ate in thoughtful silence, and when the food was gone and only the coffee was left, Connor spoke. "Are you going to give me a hard time every time I want to do something for you and Dannie?"

"Every time?" Her eyes grazed his face. "How many times will that be, Connor? After a few extravagant gifts, then what?"

"I offered you money," he reminded her quietly. "That offer still stands."

"And I offered to let you see Dannie, and if she's more than a novelty to you, that offer still stands."

Connor held his cup in both hands, studying its contents thoughtfully. "That's really all you want from me?"

Was that really more than he wanted to give? "Dannie has one very self-centered uncle and one rather eccentric mother. That's a very limited family for a little girl. You told her you were her Uncle Connor, and that's all she wants from you."

"But what do you want?"

"I want you to be careful not to make promises you can't keep, not to dazzle her with expensive gifts, not to spoil her." Too many negatives, Sarah. Give him a positive. "We don't want your money, honey, but if you've got some time..." she recited with a smile.

Connor grinned. "Got a little country in your soul after all, haven't you, Sarah Benedict?"

"I think I can match *you* hayseed for hayseed, Connor Ryan."

She watched his grin relax into a soft smile as he leaned slightly forward on his elbows and gazed across the rim of his cup at her, his eyes skylight blue. "I've got plenty of time. When can you come out and see me—both of you?"

Sarah lifted naturally delicate eyebrows over a mocking brown-eyed smile. "To California? When gas prices get back down to forty cents a gallon. To Nashville, maybe sixty cents."

"I can't send you a couple of plane tickets?" Sarah shook her head, still smiling. "They're cheap, you know, coast to coast." The head continued to shake. "Hey, what is this? I haven't always had the kind of money I have now, and this is hardly noblesse-oblige time. You know what kind of family I've got?" He set his cup down patiently, noticing that she was listening now, no longer shaking her head. "I've got parents, whom I see infrequently because we can hardly think of anything to say to each other, and I think I've got a couple of aunts and cousins somewhere, though we pretty much lost touch over the years with all the moving we did. So things are pretty limited on the Ryan side of Dannie's family, too. Sarah, I've got time *and* money on my hands. Let me spend some of it on my brother's daughter."

Oh, Lord, this man was charming and here he was in her house again. The image of the spotlighted stage star was quickly fading from Sarah's mind as she listened to him talk about family and watched him dawdle over eggs and coffee. She had to recall that party and those fish-eyed people and remember that his life-style was one that was bound to be filled with weeping and wailing and teeth gnashing. And deep down she knew the charm threatened her own peace of mind more than it did her daughter's... *her* daughter's.

"Our door is always open... to Dannie's Uncle Connor," Sarah told him quietly.

Connor took that as a rejection. Grimly admonishing himself to say no more, he remembered the offer he'd made a couple of years ago to his parents—a trip for their anniversary. They had talked about taking a cruise when, as his father had always said, "we can go in real style." Connor had consulted a travel agency and presented them some options in the form of a gift when he took them out to dinner for their wedding anniversary. The meal was a custom that Kevin and Connor had started many years ago and that Connor observed whenever possible for reasons still not quite clear to him. His father had declined the trip, assuring Connor that they were just too busy to get away. He then remembered thinking of all of his gifts that had never brought quite the pleasure that Kevin's had, and that if this had been Kevin's gift...

His watch confirmed his growing suspicion that he'd stayed long enough. He helped Sarah clear the table but made no further offers. He was ready to leave—had his jacket on, his hand on the doorknob. Another minute and she'd say something at least, give him something to take with him. He didn't want to go without... some sign of...

He was leaving, and she had no idea whether she'd see him again. A raft of suggestions raced in her head, some totally ridiculous, others totally unacceptable, but she had to say something before he was gone and it was too late.

"Connor, if you have no family commitments, maybe you'd like to come for Christmas," Sarah said quickly.

There was a bright flicker in his eyes, but it faded just as quickly. "I have . . . we have a concert in Austin—a benefit. It's going to be televised."

She smiled sadly, sensing shared disappointment. "I'll be able to see you on TV, then." And she quickly amended, "*We* will."

He dropped his hand from the doorknob now and looked at her earnestly. "I'm glad I came, Sarah. I told myself I was coming to negotiate a settlement, but if that had really been the case, I'd have sent my lawyer. I wanted to find some part of Kevin still alive. That's really why I came. There was a lot of water under the bridge between him and me, but Kevin was my brother, and he was my friend, and I miss him."

At that moment Connor looked more vulnerable than Sarah was certain Kevin had ever been. Kevin had never revealed any such personal feeling to her. She'd sometimes wondered if Kevin had ever experienced doubt or anger or pain. But Connor's eyes said that he had known all three. And Sarah, who had known them also, wanted nothing more at this moment than to reach out to Connor, to speak of Sarah and Connor, but the words failed her. She chose, instead, to affirm the one emotional cornerstone she knew they shared.

"I miss him, too," she said. I will miss you was what she wanted to say.

And I will miss you was what he wanted to hear.

Chapter Four

Can't spare a minute or a tinker's damn
Got nothin' left over for Uncle Sam
But she don't care if I'm rich or not
Cause I'm givin' my woman all I got.

Dannie, I've told you not to touch the stereo.'' Sarah sighed as she pulled the vacuum-cleaner plug from the wall. The voice on the radio was a welcome sound, displacing the empty roar of the vacuum, but Sarah resolutely pushed the warm feeling aside and persisted with the reminder, "This isn't our house."

"That's Uncle Connor's song, isn't it, Mommy?" Returning to her baby doll and its assortment of small clothes, Dannie watched the vacuum cleaner suck up its cord like a piece of spaghetti. Her mother dismantled the machine, seeming not to have heard the question. It was not until the song was over that Sarah turned the radio off and carefully closed the doors on the stereo's fine cherry-wood cabinet.

"I remember he sang that song in his show," Dannie concluded, hoping her mother would remember, too.

Sarah smiled. "Isn't it nice that we can turn the radio on and hear his voice? Not every little girl can hear her uncle's voice at the flip of a switch."

"Is that his real voice?" Dannie studied the silent cabinet. "Was he really singing at the other end of the radio?"

"No, they were playing his record at the other end. But it was his real voice on the record." If that voice gave Dannie a feeling of wonder, she had a right to it. She was not yet five years old. Sarah, on the other hand, was privately embarrassed about the pattering sensation that voice caused within her. She was really too old to be a groupie.

"Put your toys in your tote bag now, Dannie. I think Lady Lavinia's house is ready to receive guests." Pushing Connor's voice to the back of her mind, Sarah surveyed Lavinia Porter's living room. Tomorrow morning it would be strewn with empty glasses and ashtrays full of cigarette butts, and Sarah would be paid to restore it to its present condition—immaculate except for Dannie's crayons still on the side table.

Sarah picked Dannie's drawing up from the table. Dannie had taken an interest in drawing quite early on, Sarah thought, and now her shapes were recognizable. She had a real feel for color and texture. Indulging herself in a proud-mother smile, Sarah noted Dannie's rather original bent for putting things in an unexpected order; her flowers grew under the vase, and the man in profile had eyes in the back of his head. It was nice that children were free to experiment. Sarah believed in providing paper and pencil or crayons—never a coloring book, which might cramp Dannie's budding style.

A purple tote bag stuffed with doll clothes dropped at Sarah's feet. "I like these pictures very much, sweetheart," Sarah said. Dannie's tiny teeth shone brightly in her smile. "You're really into purple lately, aren't you?"

"Those are like the flowers you painted. I'm going to give them to Uncle Connor when he comes back." One by one, Dannie returned her crayons to their little box. "He likes your pictures," she reported, trying to jam a yellow crayon among its fellows. "Do you think he'll like mine?"

"I'm sure he will." On second thought she asked, "How do you know he likes my pictures?"

"He told me. Up on the mountain he said it was as pretty as one of your pictures. And he said *you're* pretty and *I'm* pretty." The yellow crayon had been jammed into the box, and she was working on an orange one. Her puffy little frown betrayed frustration, and she was grateful when Sarah took the box from her hand. Mother's magic fingers easily coaxed the crayons into straight rows, leaving space for one more, which Dannie slid into place with a triumphant smile. "And he doesn't have a little girl, except now he's got me, and he's glad he found me."

The innocent joy shimmering in Dannie's blue eyes squeezed Sarah's heart like a fruit press. "Dannie, you have to understand that Uncle Connor isn't going to be . . . he won't be able to . . ."

Wide eyes waited expectantly, innocence at the fore. "Won't be able to what, Mommy?"

Sarah brushed a stray wisp of blond hair back toward Dannie's curly ponytail. Experience would shatter her expectations all too soon. A few disappointments, a rejection or two, and this beautiful quality of childhood would be gone. "Uncle Connor lives very far from us, sweetheart. You probably won't see him . . . very often."

Dannie smiled confidently. "He lives in California. He has a horse named Ginger, and he's going to teach me how to ride it."

Promises, promises. Didn't he realize that children believed in them? "I'm sure he'd like to do that, but you must remember that California is . . . just so far away from us." Far away from us in every way possible. Light-years away.

"I know that. But airplanes take you there."

Beautiful innocence.

Through his glass wall Connor Ryan watched a white-lipped, blue-gray wave roll over his stretch of beach. The clouds overhead were steely gray, angry and anxious to release some tension. Coolness penetrated his back as he leaned against the stonework in the corner of the room where stone wall met glass wall. The stone wall housed a fireplace, which offered some sense of home, while the glass wall gave him a sense of freedom.

He had a tight-fisted hold on both ends of the towel that hung around his neck. The wall felt hard and hurt slightly, but it was cool. He'd worked himself into a heated sweat at the weight bench, sat in the sauna, showered, and now the cool stones felt good on his back.

Dropping his head back against the wall, he dragged heavily on the cigarette he held in a cupped hand and then blew a gray cloud of his own. Why did he hammer his body into shape with weights and then tear it down with cigarettes? Something gnawed at him from the inside, something like the bark-boring worms he used to find in the trunk of his tree house when he was a kid. He would poke at them and kill them because they made his tree weep in the crotch of its branches while they turned its wood to pulp. Now he would smoke out the gnawing gut borer with a smudge pot full of tobacco.

From the multitude of hidden stereo speakers, a Castilian rhythm of classical-guitar music filled the room. Pushing away from the wall on a burst of restlessness, Connor flicked the last inch of the cigarette into the cold cavern of the fireplace. He shoved a hassock aside with an impatient foot and dropped into a plush chair, swiveling it to face the sea. He'd chosen this house for its beauty and solitude, and now, as evening shadows and dark clouds drew in around him, he saw that the beauty could be hauntingly hollow and the solitude was bleak.

He'd always been a loner, but he'd never wanted to be truly alone. Kevin had known that. Scotch understood it, too, and so did Maggie. They both loved Connor, and they hoped he'd find what they had together.

Unlike Mike, he'd quickly tired of the parade of women through his bedroom, and so this kind of solitude had become more the rule of his off-tour life rather than the exception. His friends accepted that as part and parcel of his creative nature. But those close to him knew that he was lonely.

Lonely, yes, but not miserable. Not pacing with the physical ache that had plagued him since he'd come home this time. The house seemed bigger, emptier, colder than he remembered. He was surrounded by the starkness of white, and the ocean echoed endlessly. The garish painting over the fireplace had to go, and those on the opposite wall were meaningless. He wanted some warmth in this room. He wanted something of Sarah's. His hand dropped over the phone and hesitated, as it had a hundred times in the last week. He needed something of Sarah herself.

> *It's a misty river morning, babe*
> *The sun's just blinkin' through the trees*
> *White mist risin' on the lazy river's bend*
> *And white light seepin' through the window shade.*

The telephone jangled more insistently than usual, and now Sarah set brush and palette pad aside in disgust, gave her hands a cursory wipe on a rag and picked up the receiver. "Sarah Benedict," she clipped, reaching to turn down the volume on the radio.

"Sarah Benedict, you gorgeous struggling artist you, this is Barbara from the Tate Gallery. Are you deaf, Sarah? I've been calling all morning, and I know your schedule. You're home on Wednesdays."

"I'm home, but I'm working. What's up, Barbara?"

"What's up? Not you, I hope. You'd better be sitting down. I've got news, lady. Big-bucks news."

Barbara Tate should have owned a football team rather than an art gallery. Over the phone she always rattled the eardrum with her news, which was always couched in a directive. Sarah simply waited quietly for the point.

"We sold three of your paintings yesterday out of the clear blue. You won't believe this, Sarah. The *price* we got is unbelievable! And, of course, my commission is wonderful. We're on our way."

Sold three pieces all at once? Sarah let that sink in before she got to the next part. "What kind of unbelievable price?"

"Three grand!" The two syllables burst over the wires. "Can you believe it? *Three* grand."

"Which ones?" Astonishment gave way to ecstasy. "Who bought them?"

"Let's see ... *Apple-Pickers*, *Girl by the Pond* and *Destinations*. Great pieces, Sarah. Wonderful work. He wanted earthiness—bronze, sienna, gold—with soft-color accents."

"Who? Who wanted ... ?"

"Some broker from California. I must be advertising better than I thought. Bought them for some rock star, I guess."

Oh, Connor, you didn't! "Did you *ask* for a thousand dollars apiece, Barbara?"

"No, no, Sarah, he paid *three* thousand apiece. And I should tell you I got it for you, but I didn't. He offered two, and when my mouth dropped open, he said three was his final offer. And he wanted Sarah Benedict, no one else. The word must be out on you at last, my friend. I didn't know you were showing anything out on the West Coast."

"I'm not. I think it's someone I've . . . met."

"The broker?"

"No, the . . . uh . . . the musician." Sarah really didn't want to get into this, certainly not with Barbara.

"A rock star? *You?*"

"He's sort of a friend of a friend. A friend's relative, actually. Look, Barbara, this isn't real. I mean, this man is very eccentric, and I'm sure he doesn't intend . . ."

"The money's real, Sarah. It's in my hand."

"But it's a fluke. It doesn't set any precedents."

"Maybe this guy'll tell all his eccentric friends what a good deal he got. Let's hope so. Check's in the mail. Have some fun with it. I'm raising your prices. Bye, now."

Raising her prices! She'd probably never sell anything again, thanks to Connor Ryan. Sarah stared down at the assortment of colors on her palette, at odds with herself. She should have been happy about the sale. She wanted to be; she had waited long enough for one like this. But this wasn't the way it was supposed to work. The buyer was supposed to be convinced he'd found the next Picasso. It wasn't supposed to be conscience money. And what was she doing on Connor Ryan's conscience, anyway? Dannie wasn't his child.

But Dannie talked about him all the time, and Sarah thought about him more than she wanted to. He crept into her dreams at night and haunted her during the day. She could have excused these feelings if she could honestly have believed it was because he'd brought Kevin back, but she knew it wasn't the memory of that. Her mind was filled with Connor.

You and me and the river, babe,
Makin' misty morning love.

"Sarah, it's Connor."

"Connor." The name was caressed in soft surprise.

"The paintings are beautiful."

"They should be. You paid handsomely for them."

"Not enough. Not nearly. The colors are perfect here—warm and muted. I have a thing about color, and I like the way you use it."

"I'm glad you like them, but I wish you'd just paid what they were worth. Then I might believe you weren't just patronizing me."

She bristled at his soft laugh. It seemed indulgent. "Sarah, all the great artists were patronized. Michelangelo had a patron, didn't he? You shouldn't be scrubbing floors when you could be doing what you do so beautifully."

"Maybe I like scrubbing floors." She knew that sounded like a juvenile retort, but he had no business making judgments about her livelihood.

"Yeah. Maybe I liked pumping gas and busing tables. You're talking to someone who knows all about it, kid. I like to make music, and you like to paint, and it's great to get paid for doing what you like to do. How's Dannie?"

"Dannie's fine. She likes having a new uncle. She recognizes your songs when they play them on the radio. I bought her a record the other day, and she plays it all the time."

"On what?"

"On her little record player."

"I bet we sound less than great on a kiddie-time record player. You girls need a decent stereo. I'll see that—"

"No, Connor. Please. We're not your special charity. Your brother wasn't using your ID when he met me."

"My ID? Oh…yeah." He remembered making some remark about people coming after him for favors. "That was a joke, Sarah. You've more than convinced me that you weren't looking for anything. In fact, I'm beginning to wonder if I'm to be allowed *any* privileges. I want to be . . ." He couldn't say what he wanted to be. He didn't know yet. He knew he wanted to be in the same room with her right now instead of at the other end of a telephone cable. "I want to help."

"You have. You've almost convinced me that one of my paintings could be worth three thousand dollars."

There was a smile in her voice, and it put one in his. "I have them hanging up, and they've already appreciated in value. I've already gotten my money's worth. They give the place a whole different feeling."

"I'm glad. *Apple Pickers* is one of my favorites, and I'm glad it went to someone who'll enjoy it. And it *will* be worth a great deal more someday, I promise."

"I do have a problem with them, though." The suggestion was delicately scented bait for his hook.

"What's that?"

"They make the rest of the stuff I've got hanging around here look like dime-store junk. I took down that thing I had over the fireplace. Couldn't stand it anymore. What have you got that's about four feet by five feet?"

"My kitchen table."

He laughed again, and this time she tingled at the sound. "Come on, Sarah, I'm in trouble here. I'm doing my own thing, and I want to do it right. When it's all done, I plan to invite that decorator lady over and give her a taste of real class."

Sarah tried not to wonder anything about this "decorator lady." "Really, Connor, I have nothing that big. I don't think I've ever stretched a canvas that size."

"You could, though."

"Yes, I could, but I haven't any plans for anything that large. Maybe your broker should..."

"What you could do is come out and look the place over. Kind of get an idea of where it would go, what the setting's like."

"Go out to California?" The idea was absurd.

"Sure. Bring Dannie. She'll love it here. I hope she hasn't learned to swim yet because I want to be the one to teach her. And she can—"

"Hold it! Hold it right there, Connor." Sarah quickly swallowed any wistfulness that might betray regret and declared a firm, "We can't do that."

"Why not? Don't give me any nonsense about the price of gas. I'll send plane tickets."

"I can't just pick up and leave any time I want, Connor. I have obligations."

"Anytime you *want*," he repeated, examining the words. "That means you want to come, but the people of Amherst can't clean their own houses for a week or so."

"It means," she clarified, "that I plan our vacations months in advance, that I put money aside for them and that I buy my own tickets. I'm wary of eccentric musicians who spread their money around so freely, Mr. Ryan."

"Good God, you're methodical." He sighed. "Whatever happened to eccentric artists?"

"They learned from Michelangelo's example. Patrons have a way of coming up with the most unreasonable demands," Sarah explained.

"And you're thinking if I ask you to spend some time lying on your back, it won't be to paint the ceiling of any chapel," he assumed in a humorless tone of voice.

Sarah felt her face grow hot. "I'm not thinking that at all," she said quietly.

"I'm not thinking that way, either. I'm thinking I like your work, and I'd like to own more of it. I'm thinking..." He took a deep breath. "I'm thinking I want to see you and Dannie again, but if I tell you that and you turn me down... I'm thinking maybe you should think it over, Sarah. I'm not looking for favors from you any more than you want favors from me. Let's put that illusion to rest and see what's left, okay? You give it some thought."

Sarah replaced the receiver in its cradle with deliberate care. This man confused her as no man ever had before. He lived a fast-paced, glamorous life. Men like that were supposed to be interested in fast, glamorous women, certainly not in a mother and child.

Since Kevin, Sarah had dated only occasionally. She had a child to consider. There were times when Sarah worried about Dannie growing up without a father, times when she felt the burden of her many roles, and she thought that burdens were meant to be shared. There were many times when Sarah reasoned that a comfortable, dependable, secure relationship with a man might not be a bad idea.

But Sarah's thoughts had taken a new tack lately. There were times when she felt terribly alone, and she needed to be close, to touch, to share herself. Those were the times when there was no logic or reason or decision. There was only an uncontrollable longing of the heart and an image of Connor. This man attracted her as no man ever had before.

For pure and unlimited exasperation power, no man could beat Sarah's brother. He'd been hanging around the house for three days and showed no sign of leaving. Sarah had planned to keep the news of her big sale a secret, but the cat was out of the bag when he took a follow-up call from Barbara at the gallery. The news gave Jerry a sudden spurt of energy, which he directed to a relentless pursuit of happiness in Sarah's behalf.

"You know, I've never felt quite right about moving out of here and leaving you and Dannie all alone. You need a man around here, Sarah."

Sarah eyed Jerry's clumsy attempt to trim carrots and wondered how soon he'd cut himself. "I take it Pepper hasn't forgiven you yet."

"In her heart, she probably has. She just hasn't got the words out yet." Jerry tipped his head back thoughtfully, allowing himself a brief mental workout. The look that followed was meant to forewarn her that he'd arrived at a weighty conclusion. "I think it's time I came home, Sarah. I've been shirking my duties where you and Dannie are concerned. Pepper is just—" he shrugged, turning his mouth down in casual dismissal "—just a passing fling. You and Dannie are family."

What had she done to deserve this? Sold some paintings? Cooked his favorite dinner? Either one would have done it for Jerry. "You're family, too, Jerry. We love you. You can stay one more night. Tomorrow you're going to call Pepper and let her get the words out."

"No, I mean it Sarah."

"Of course, you could get an apartment of your own." She cocked him a sweet smile.

"You're not as nice as you used to be, Sarah. Spinsterhood is making a mean old lady out of you. You're going to have warts on your nose and start cackling pretty soon." With the end of a carrot he indicated a likely spot at the tip of her nose. "Do yourself a favor. Take a trip out to California."

"I should never have told you. I can't imagine why he'd even suggest it."

"The man's crazy about you. He must be. Why else would he pay nine thousand dollars for three little pictures?"

"Obviously he knows good art. Cut those into sticks, please." Sarah slid a roasting pan from the oven, inhaling the sweet, cured aroma as the drippings from the ham popped their last. "Then you can slice this."

"Ouch! Damn. Cut myself. Take over for me here, would you? I'm bleeding." The look on Jerry's face asked for pity, and she gave it as she would to any wounded, helpless thing.

It was easy to feel sorry for him. Their mother always had, and with her death just three years ago, the care and feeding of Jerry had been left to the women in his life who had a soft spot for wounded, helpless things. Their father, it seemed, had been gone forever. He'd left them for the lure of a more glamorous life as an actor and now and then turned up on a soap opera.

"I'm not good for much, am I, Sarah?"

Here it came. Jerry was going to hand her a little self-pity along with the knife and cutting board. Sarah returned a raised brow and no comment.

"No, I mean it. I never seem to be in the right place at the right time with the right idea." He smiled, and Sarah knew it was that smile that got him all he wanted. "I did write a damned good letter, though. And it turned out even better than I thought. He's a nice guy, Sarah." He laid a brotherly hand on Sarah's shoulder. "Take that trip. Don't think about it. Just do it."

Our love's a melancholy used-to-be
My cellar full of faded memories
The dusty echoes of a lie
A lonely, hollow, aching sigh
A room where nothing stands but me.

The idea came to him all in one piece when Connor paid his obligatory visit to his parents. He wondered, almost idly, what they'd say to news of a grandchild—a child of Kevin's flesh. Curiosity got the best of him, and he tried it out on them. They loved it. They wanted to meet her. He knew they meant to bring Kevin back through his child, and that was natural. He'd wanted that himself in a way; he knew that now.

Then he'd met Sarah and her daughter, and things had changed. She wasn't "Kevin's kid" anymore; she was Dannie. She was the princess who could wrap her arms around his neck, call him "Uncle Connor" and make his heart swell. And the woman in the picture he'd carried in his pocket had become Sarah—delicate and shy and warm. If she wanted to, she could split his heart wide open.

The idea was to get them here.

"Sarah, it's Connor."

"Hello, Connor." She really hadn't expected him to call again.

"I have a proposition for you."

No preliminaries. This was definitely not Kevin. Sarah cradled the receiver against her ear and tightened her other hand around the mouthpiece. "An offer I can't refuse?"

"I'm sure you can, knowing you. Here it is anyway: Dannie's grandparents want to meet her. They live in San Francisco. I don't know whether I told you, but Kevin was kind of larger than life for them. I told them about Dannie because...well, I thought they had a right to know."

Kevin was larger than life? What was Connor, then? "Of course they did. Were they shocked?"

Connor considered for a moment. "I guess they went through a range of reactions. They're saddened by the tragedy that Kevin died before he knew about his child—before he was able to marry you. But they're glad to have a grandchild. They figure I won't come through for them."

"Of course, a man in your position has to be careful."

"Of course." Was she actually teasing him? "They really want to meet her, Sarah. They deserve that much, don't you think? Let me send the tickets."

"San Francisco?"

"Yes."

"When?"

"Whenever you say."

A moment's deliberation, and then a sigh. "All right. Dannie deserves that much, too."

Connor smiled at the soft-colored painting that hung on the wall above him. Stroke of genius, Ryan. Whoever said you weren't that bright?

Chapter Five

Sarah had never flown first-class. It was an experience in luxury and decadence, she decided, looking over the luncheon menu. No hamburgers and fries. What was a four-year-old supposed to eat? *Boeuf Bourguignonne?* A glance at Dannie's wonder-lit face told Sarah that whatever this plane had to offer would suit her just fine. Sarah soon found herself sipping at a perpetually full glass of champagne and deciding that luxury and decadence had their good points. The pilot suggested they prepare for landing before Sarah fully realized she was flying.

She was feeling a bit foolish when she walked into the terminal, flight bag on one shoulder, Dannie's hand firmly clutched in her other hand. Her heart fluttered in her throat as she scanned the canvas of faces. She attributed her anxiety strictly to schoolgirl silliness.

Where was he? Did he send someone to pick them up, someone she wouldn't recognize? Did he remember the time, the flight number, or did he have a secretary to take care of all the worrisome little details in his life? Did some strange woman make the reservations, buy the—

"There he is, Mommy! Uncle Connor! See?"

Sarah lost control of her face's inane grin, and suddenly the absurdity she felt didn't matter anymore. He was smiling, too, behind a pair of dark glasses. There were barriers—people, a railing, a cart full of luggage—but some means of propulsion totally unconnected to her body carried her to him quickly. At a distance of three feet she stopped short and caught her breath, still beaming. She wanted to walk right into him, but she caught herself in time. Instead, she stared at the honey-tan face and tousled blond hair. Could he have been in a hurry to get here?

He wanted to hold her, but his arms stiffened awkwardly at his sides. He knew he was grinning like a Cheshire cat, and he couldn't help that. The instructions he'd given himself when he heard them announce her flight number—stay cool, look casual, sort of like, "Oh, you're here already?"—had been useless. She looked every bit as good as he remembered. He'd been planning to get her out in the sun, but maybe he shouldn't. That porcelain face was so translucent, so refined that it demanded to be pampered. Her hair hung soft and loose, and her brown eyes glistened. She didn't look like a woman who'd had her arm twisted over the phone.

"Great to see you, Sarah," he offered, and wished immediately it had sounded different.

Broadening her grin, she reached for the sunglasses and removed them from his face. He didn't flinch. "Great to see you, too, Connor." The low purr was not something she recognized as her own sound. She slipped the glasses in the front pocket of his blue blazer.

"Just one of the trappings," he explained.

"Trappings," she mused. "Yes, you seem to be an expert. The prey is even pleased to be here."

"Prey?" His smile become cocky. "I invited you here, polite as you please. You accepted."

"Yes, I did. And you didn't even have to mention the champagne."

"You started without me?"

"Started what?"

The smile melted, and the answer came first through his eyes. "The celebration, Sarah." They reached for each other in slow motion, and he repeated, "The celebration."

Dannie wasn't sure what to make of all this. She had the feeling she'd almost been forgotten, but the looks her mother and her uncle were giving each other felt warm, even from her perspective. It didn't surprise her when they stopped grinning and gabbing at each other and finally kissed. It sure seemed like a long kiss, though, and Dannie wondered if she'd get one, too.

"Uncle Connor?"

The little voice rapped at the perimeter of Connor's brain, which was bubbling with the taste of champagne. It took a supreme effort to drag his lips away from Sarah's, and his "Hmm" was more groan than question.

"I want a kiss, too."

The cherubic face smiled up at him, and he remembered himself. Without completely relinquishing his hold on Sarah, he scooped Dannie up in one arm, bringing their three faces within a nose length of one another. He gave Dannie a quick, hard, noisy kiss that left her frowning with confusion. "How come you kissed Mommy bigger than you kissed me?"

He laughed and bussed her once more on the cheek. "Because that's the way it's supposed to be, Princess. A big girl like your mom just gets one big kiss." The arm around Sarah's waist tightened in a reassuring squeeze as he pecked Dannie again, this time on her nose. "Little girls get a bunch of little kisses." Another peck had her giggling with delight. "You can have all you want," he promised with a firm kiss on her forehead. "You say when. I'm really glad to see you, you know."

Sarah watched them smile at each other. The resemblance between the two profiles was remarkable. He was good for Dannie, she thought. She'd done the right thing in bringing her here.

"I guess Uncle Jerry doesn't know about different kisses," Dannie said. "He kisses me and Mommy both the same."

Connor dropped a glance at Sarah before pursuing. "Really?"

"He kisses little kisses," Sarah explained. "One each."

"Ah." Connor nodded, his eyes dancing from one face to the other and back again. "That's probably because Jerry doesn't understand the code of chivalry. He isn't a true knight."

"Are you a knight, Uncle Connor?"

"I'm a Georgia Night," he confided secretively. "We spell it a little differently, but then I never had much respect for spelling. I know a real princess when I see one. Ready to meet your grandparents?"

"Will they know a real princess when they see one?" Sarah asked.

"They can't wait. I've told them how you feel about spoiling her, but I don't think it did much good. They're crazy about her already." There was a kind of longing in Connor's eyes, a need that Sarah couldn't identify. "Thanks for letting me give them this, Sarah." Then it was as though he caught himself being too serious, and he shrugged it off with half a laugh. "It's your doing, of course, but I'm a hell of a facilitator. Don't you agree?"

Sarah gave him the warm smile she thought he needed. "You're a true knight, Connor Ryan."

Connor's parents lived in a stylish San Francisco apartment that boasted a lovely view of the city. The family resemblance was so strong that Sarah believed she'd have recognized his father if she'd met him on the street. If his hair had been allowed to grow, it would have been full and thick and completely white, but he wore it in a crew cut, as she imagined he had when it was the same straw color he'd given his sons. Even in retirement, the man was regulation army. His stature, his dress, the very expression on his face was command-ing. He offered Sarah a hearty handshake.

"Connor has told us the whole story. We're pleased, Miss Benedict. We're very pleased."

Connor's mother's voice was too melodious ever to be an intrusion. Its softness held the memory of a Southern upbringing, and the hug she greeted Sarah with was regulation would-be mother-in-law. "It should have been Mrs. Ryan, and if Kevin had lived—" Sarah was held at arm's length now, the woman's soft blue eyes intense with sincerity "—if Kevin had lived, he would have made it so."

Sarah could see this was not the time to suggest al-ternatives. "I know. But I'd still be Sarah." She smiled that assurance at them both.

Roberta Ryan nodded and squeezed Sarah's arms before she released her and turned to Connor, who held the prize in his arms. "Where's the little girl who's going to call me Grandma? Where's my little . . . oooh, Dwight, look. She's the image of Kevin." She held ea-ger hands up to Dannie, who took a firmer hold on Connor's neck while she sized the woman up. "Will you come to see your grandma, Danielle? I've been waiting a long time to give you a hug."

Dannie looked first to her mother, then to Connor, who explained, "This is your grandmother, Dannie. Remember, I told you before that she was your dad's mother, and she's my mother. That makes her your grandmother."

Dannie checked the woman out again. She had no experience with grandmothers, and the grandma who talked about cookies on TV looked a lot different.

"Your daddy was my little boy, honey, my baby."

"You're my Uncle Connor's mommy?"

The woman nodded, smiling anxiously. She had gray hair like a grandma, but she didn't have too many wrinkles, and she didn't have glasses, and she was almost as thin as Dannie's own mother. Dannie liked almost everything about her, except she had long red fingernails. Dannie didn't like those at all. She decided to stay right where she was.

"Give her a little time, Mom," Connor suggested, reassuring Dannie with a pat on the back. "She'll let you know when she's ready for that hug. Right, Princess?"

Dannie agreed with a nod, and Roberta backed off, turning to her husband. "I can't get over how much she looks like Kevin. Doesn't she look just like Kevin?"

"She does," Dwight Ryan confirmed. Dannie's curious look prompted him to offer, "I'm your grandfather, young lady."

"And he's not as mean as he looks," Roberta put in, reaching for Sarah's hand. "He'll always be a soldier—all spit and polish on the first meeting. You know how they are, Sarah. I thought we'd have dinner a little early, since your stomachs are probably still on Eastern time. Connor will put your bags in the guest room. You just get comfortable, now, and we'll give Danielle time to warm up to us." Roberta led the way to the living room, where Connor joined her in his preferred spot beside her on the couch. Dannie crawled over to her mother's lap.

"Would you like a drink, Sarah?" Dwight asked, his tone losing its formal edge. When Sarah declined, he made Connor the same offer.

"Not unless you have a beer, Dad."

"When are you going to start drinking a *man's* drink? Whiskey and water is a man's drink."

"When are you going to put a beer in the refrigerator for me when you know I'm coming over?"

"One of these days I'll remember. Put that on your shopping list next time, Bobbie," Dwight ordered, sliding open a door on the liquor cabinet.

Sarah glanced at Connor in time to see his eyes glaze over, and she remembered that whiskey and water was Kevin's drink.

It was Dannie who smoothed over the evening's awkward edges. Within a few minutes, she ventured away from the couch, which became home base, and she began prowling the room. The room's decor had an Oriental flavor, and Dannie found lots of pretty things to examine. She'd been in Sarah's clients' living rooms often enough to know that you had to be careful with other people's things. A lacquered Japanese music box caught her attention, and Roberta happily showed her its workings. They smiled at each other as the box played "China Nights," and the pretty woman with the fashionably short gray haircut and the crystal-blue eyes became Dannie's grandma.

Throughout the evening, there was talk of the army. Dwight Ryan reveled in it. Roberta put in her reminiscences of faraway places and people who'd been stationed with them here and had turned up again there.

Sarah listened, offering a memory or two of Wiesbaden, which was about all she knew of the army.

Connor found himself reverting to an old tactic. After turning off the lights in his brain and pulling down all the shades, he was able to nod or offer a word or two occasionally without allowing the insignificance of his presence to bother him. The talk was of the army and of Kevin and the old man. The focus was on Kevin's child and the woman whom Kevin had loved. Why had Connor expected anything different? He'd only brought them here.

As dinner wound down to apple pie and coffee, Dwight wondered aloud whether Sarah had seen Kevin's "chopper" up close.

"Yes, I did once," she said. "Kevin took me to an open house once—Armed Forces Day, I believe."

"What did you think of it?" Dwight asked.

"I loved the parade. The band and all the uniforms and the close-order marching."

"I mean the big bird," Dwight clarified. "What did you think of that?"

Sarah's stomach tightened. What did she think of the machine that had taken Kevin to his death? "It was...very big. Much bigger than I had imagined." She didn't care to remember any more than that.

Unexpectedly, Dwight chuckled. "Big. Damn right, it was big. I used to kid him about being a fly-boy instead of a *real* soldier, but we both knew what kind of soldier he was. And he went down like a soldier. You didn't know anything about his mission, did you, Sarah?"

"No," Sarah said quietly.

"Of course not. He was a soldier."

Connor's brain activated, his jaw tightening as he focused on Sarah's discomfort. "They wouldn't tell us anything, either, Dad."

"He was shot down by enemy fire," Dwight said.

"We don't know that."

"I know it. He was a soldier." Father's eyes caught son's, and there was an unmistakable judgment in them. "Like his father. All man, one hundred percent. *A soldier*."

The words had been thrown back and forth so often that they had become unnecessary. The space surrounding the stare-down was electric with the old dispute. The army had sent Dwight Ryan the honored remains of a heroic son. To Connor it had returned a dead brother.

"My father's name was Kevin, and he was killed in the war."

Eye contact between the two men snapped almost audibly as each turned toward the little voice. "You see? The child knows. Instinctively, she knows," Dwight insisted.

"She knows he's not here," Connor said gently. "She knows she's never..."

Dannie flashed a grin at her grandfather. "Mommy painted a picture of him, and it looks just like Uncle Connor. And I look like Uncle Connor, too. Uncle Connor sings on the radio. I just turn the radio on, and after a while he sings."

Connor felt his heart grow inside his chest.

"We went to see his show, too," Dannie announced, turning to her mother for support. "Didn't we, Mommy?"

"Yes, we did," Sarah confirmed, silently marveling at her daughter's diplomatic timing. "We sat in the front row." Looking to Roberta for a contribution, she offered, "It must be so exciting for you to watch your son perform before a huge crowd. He has quite a following."

"Actually, we don't . . . the loud music and the wild crowds can be so unnerving, and Dwight doesn't . . ."

"Teenagers," Dwight mumbled. "Screaming idiots, most of them."

"We went to one," Roberta amended quickly. "But it was so nerve-racking. I was afraid they might tear his clothes off before the night was over. Of course, we have all the records."

"I know very little about music," Sarah admitted, "popular or otherwise. And crowds make me uncomfortable, too. But it's easy to understand why the crowd gets a little rowdy at a Georgia Nights concert." Turning to Connor, Sarah indicated that her comments to his mother were really for him now. "I've been listening to their music, paying more attention to the medium and the message. The medium is different from mine, but the message . . . the message isn't so different."

Connor smiled across the table at her and let the rest of the room drift out of focus. "No, it's not so different. But your statements are much softer."

"There's more excitement in yours," she countered. "Your colors are bolder."

"But there's quiet excitement in yours, Sarah. That softness creates a yearning for... for softness." The tinkle of "China Nights" pulled Connor's attention back into the room, and he offered his mother part of the smile he'd given Sarah, part of the good feeling her compliments had stirred. "My music may not be your style, Mom, but you'd like Sarah's paintings, I'm sure. See for yourself next time you come down. I intend to have a much bigger collection by then."

"It seems there's a sudden big-name demand for my work," Sarah reminded him. "Prices have skyrocketed."

"I'm planning to beat the run on Sarah Benedicts by commissioning a couple of pieces. So you know what you're getting for Christmas, Mom."

"How nice!" Roberta exclaimed. "I'm sure I'd love..."

"You really would, Mom. Sarah's work is quiet, understated—sort of like some of this Japanese stuff, only it's..." Connor leaned toward his mother as his conviction grew in intensity. She'd like this gift.

"Did you really do a portrait of Kevin, Sarah?" Roberta asked.

"Yes, I did. It really isn't very..."

"I don't suppose you'd want to part with it. But maybe you could do another—a copy. I'd love a copy of Kevin's portrait."

Connor settled back on the couch, ignoring Sarah's response to his mother's request. It was no longer his gift. It was Sarah's and Kevin's. Connor had hit the nail on the head when he'd termed himself "a hell of a facilitator." His attention wandered to the corner where

Dannie had been playing with the music box, and he saw that she was stretched out beside it, sound asleep. Putting the rest of the room behind him, he went to her, carefully lifted her in his arms and carried her into the guest room.

Sarah waited a few minutes before she followed him. Something in the tenderness of his gesture had mesmerized her. He'd assumed this duty without discussion. Kevin was still here in the middle of those who remembered him, but Dannie did not remember. Dannie needed someone to put her to bed, and Connor was there.

Connor never stayed in his parents' home when he visited them. He preferred a hotel to the guest room. He surprised his mother with his announcement that he'd sleep on the couch in the den, and she let slip that this was certainly unusual for him. But Sarah had stood in the doorway and watched as Connor removed each shoe and sock from Dannie's feet. She'd handed him a little pink nightgown without comment, and he'd undressed the child and slipped the nightgown on her without disturbing her sleep at all, as though he'd done this every night for the last four-and-a-half years. Sarah knew why he'd stayed. And the thought of how he'd tucked Dannie under the puffed coverlet and kissed the top of her head before he'd slipped quietly from the room filled Sarah's head after everyone had gone to bed.

A sliver of light was visible beneath the den's closed door. Sarah tapped twice, very quietly.

"Come in," Connor's voice invited. She was still dressed in her slim tweed skirt and soft red blouse, but she'd shed the matching jacket, and her legs and feet were bare. He'd made himself comfortable, too, tossing off his tie and rolling up his shirt sleeves before lighting up a cigarette. "Is your room comfortable?" he asked. "I can probably find you another blanket if you need one."

"No, everything's fine." She moved toward him slowly, not sure why she'd come. She gestured toward the couch before she sat down, tucking one leg under her. "But this doesn't look long enough for you. I think I've taken the bed you should have."

"I don't stay here as a rule. I just didn't feel like looking for a room tonight. Should have seen to it earlier." He took a last drag on his cigarette and stubbed it out.

"Why don't you take the other bed in the guest room and let me have the couch? I'm shorter."

He considered the concerned look on her face for a moment, and it occurred to him that she was trying to make up for something someone else had done—something she'd stumbled into and didn't fully understand. He should have introduced her to Kevin's parents and left. He didn't want her thinking any of this bothered him. "I can sleep anywhere," he assured her. "Airports, buses, hotel-room floors. When you travel with a band, you become a flexible sleeper."

Sarah watched her hands smooth the taut wool fabric over her knees. "They haven't accepted Kevin's death, have they?"

He sighed. "They haven't accepted it as the total waste that it was—that *I* think it was. Time stopped the day Kevin died, and nothing's changed for them since then. Five years later, they don't even know who I am."

Sarah noticed a display of photographs on the wall of shelves behind them. Connor and Kevin. As youngsters, they looked like a pair of bookends, but as they grew older, there were marked differences in style and expression. Kevin continued to be bright and shiny faced, hair trimmed above his collar and shorter still in uniform. Connor's expression said that he'd been dragged to the photographer's studio. His hair became rebelliously long, and there were no pictures of him beyond the age of about eighteen. But there was a progression of poses of Kevin in uniform beside other pictures of a young Dwight also in uniform. The display told an interesting story. "Your father identified with Kevin's ambitions, but not with yours."

"There's more to it than that. Kevin was our bridge." Connor thought the image over and cocked half a smile at its appropriateness. "The army blew up our bridge. Left a hell of a mess."

"Is that what you hoped Dannie would be?" Sarah wondered gently. "Are you trying to rebuild?"

"No." Connor frowned a bit, and then he shook his head at the thought. "No, I'm not using Dannie. I only meant to bring them together."

"That's what Jerry said he was doing when he wrote to you," Sarah remembered. "He just wanted to get some people together."

"There's nothing wrong with that. I'm glad he did. Sarah..." He reached for her hand. It felt cool in his. "I'm really glad he did."

Sarah smiled. "I am, too."

He wanted to take her in his arms, but he couldn't do that here. There was too much of Kevin here.

Sarah went back to the guest room wondering why Connor hadn't given her the kiss she'd seen in his eyes.

The five of them spent the following day together touring San Francisco. Dannie loved the cable cars, and she squealed with delight over the hills. Connor watched his father warm up to the little girl and his mother fuss over her, and he felt good. He felt as though he'd accomplished something, and he was standing back to admire his work. He felt good, too, because Sarah seemed to have taken a place standing back beside him. Feeling this way, he could spare more patience than usual on his parents.

By the third day of their visit, Dannie had added Grandpa and Grandma to her growing family. Grandma's red fingernails didn't bother her anymore, and she found that she could get around Grandpa's stern facade with a certain kind of a smile. Grandma would fix her whatever she wanted for breakfast, but she stalled, waiting for Uncle Connor to come to the table before she committed herself.

"I'll have what Uncle Connor has," she decided, scrambling for the chair next to the one she knew he would take.

Sarah set placemats and silverware in front of each chair. Hesitating on a fork, she knew before she looked up that he was standing in the doorway and that she'd been waiting for him as surely as Dannie had.

"Good morning, ladies."

"Good morning."

"Uncle Connor, Grandma will fix us whatever we want for breakfast. What do we want? Do we want French toast?"

"As long as you've got Grandma right where we want her, I guess we should take advantage of it." Connor peeked around the island of cupboards. "Good morning, Mom. We want French toast."

"It's been a long time, honey, but I think I can manage."

On his way to the table, Connor picked up the coffeepot. "Coffee, Sarah?"

"Yes, please."

He poured for them both and then took the chair beside Dannie. "What would you two like to do today? I could tag along on a shopping trip if you'd like, or maybe..."

"Can we ride the trolley again?" Dannie asked.

"Again?" Connor and Sarah exclaimed simultaneously.

"Oh, yes! I love going up the hills and down the hills." Connor caught Sarah rolling her eyes, and he thought better of laughing. "It's just like the little train that kept thinking she could, and then she tried and then she did. Do you know that story, Uncle Connor?"

"I think I do—I think I do—I think I do." His chugging made her giggle, and he ruffled her curls in response. "There are lots of other things I want to show you, Princess. With this great streak of weather we've been having, we can go beachcombing."

"Beachcombing?" Dannie looked puzzled. "Do you have to have a special comb?"

Roberta walked in on the laughter with a newspaper in one hand and a tray of glasses of juice in the other. "You're in the paper again, Connor. Who's the girl this time?"

Sarah's chin snapped up a little too quickly for her own liking as she watched Roberta hand her son the folded paper. He flipped it over to the front page and nodded at the tabloid's masthead.

"Why do you read this thing, Mom? It's written by monkeys playing with typewriters."

"I read it to find out what my son is up to." She reached for the paper and flipped it back to the picture in question. "Who's this Marlene?" she asked, pointing to the picture.

Connor gave a quick glance and then shrugged as he claimed a glass of orange juice. "It says she was at the concert in Buffalo last month. She must be Marlene from Buffalo."

"You've got your arm around her in the picture. Did you read what else it says?" Roberta took the paper. "Just read what else it says. 'Connor Ryan, the ever-elusive bachelor of Georgia Nights fame, was more than attentive to Miss Buffalo, Marlene—'"

The paper was snatched from her hands as Connor rose abruptly from his chair. "I can read, Mom," he said quietly. "Anything I want to read, I'll read myself. Don't *ever* read to me."

Roberta lowered her eyes. "I'm sorry, Connor."

He relaxed visibly, muscle by muscle, and finally handed the paper back to his mother. "Me, too. Mostly because I smell something burning."

"The French toast!" she exclaimed, and she made a beeline for the kitchen.

Connor returned to his coffee and when Roberta brought the French toast to the table, helped Dannie cut hers up. But the scene had left Sarah considerably more shaken than she wanted to admit. Whoever Marlene was, she was none of Sarah's business. She made a tight wad of her paper napkin. Miss Buffalo, was it?

Chapter Six

I want to take you and Dannie to Santa Cruz for a few days—to my place.''

Sarah looked up from the ponytail she was making on the side of Dannie's hair. Connor shouldered the door-jamb, hands tucked in the front pockets of his jeans. He was the picture of boredom.

"Can we go beachcombing, Uncle Connor?"

Grinning, Connor hunkered down to Dannie's level. She was his natural ally. "We can go beachcombing and horseback riding and anything else you want to do, Princess."

"Ride real horses?" Dannie bounced on the balls of her feet, and Sarah lost a handful of hair. "Oh, boy, real horses!"

"Hold your real horses until I give this one its tails," Sarah ordered.

Connor lifted his eyes to the face above Dannie's. "We can go hiking in the woods, too," he promised. "And anything else your mom wants to do. *Anything.* I've got a case of cabin fever like you wouldn't believe."

"But Dannie's here to get to know her grandparents," Sarah reminded him, pulling the elastic hair tie to make a second loop.

Connor straightened slowly, and Sarah's eyes followed his until she was looking up. "I suppose you're going to tell me it isn't necessary for me to hang around any longer," he guessed. "Or you could take the more tactful approach—say you don't want to take up any more of my time."

"Actually, I was going to thank you for staying. Your being here has made this visit easier for me." Her eyes told him she knew it hadn't been easy for him. "Don't leave without us."

"Then you'll come?"

"We do want to see redwoods," Sarah said thoughtfully.

"Lots of 'em," he promised.

"And real horses," Dannie added.

"With real tails," he said, giving one of hers a little tug.

"You'll have to engineer a graceful exit." Sarah honestly had the feeling that Dwight and Roberta Ryan could probably use a rest from their energetic granddaughter, but they weren't likely to admit that yet.

"Exits are my speciality. Finish with a flourish." With a playful chuck under her chin, Connor gave Sarah another promise. "You'll love it, Sarah. It's your kind of place. Your kind of peace and quiet. And your best colors."

Connor's flourish was dinner on Fisherman's Wharf. He wrinkled his nose at Sarah's Oysters Rockefeller, but he enjoyed his shrimp, and he helped Dannie crack her crab legs. His disclosure of plans to take Sarah and Dannie on a side trip brought a moment of awkward surprise from his parents.

"But . . . where will they stay, Connor?"

"At my house, Mom. I have plenty of room for guests." He gave her an indulgent smile. "Don't worry. The accommodations will be perfectly respectable."

"I hope so. Sarah isn't one of your . . ."

Sarah stiffened against the back of her chair.

"Uncle Connor's going to let me ride a real horse," Dannie put in, and Sarah silently thanked her for another timely interruption. "And we're going to comb the beach."

"Don't you let this child get too near that water, Connor. Those waves can be . . ."

"I'll see to Dannie's safety," Connor assured her with practiced patience.

Dwight reached across the corner of the table to give Dannie a fond pat on the head. "She'll make a fine horseman. Her dad was."

"Her uncle *is*," Connor said quietly. Let it go, he told himself. Say the things they want to hear. The competition was over long ago. "We had some great times when we lived in Texas, didn't we, Dad?"

"You boys chased each other from one end of the state to the other on those two Shetlands you had."

"If you can ride a Shetland, you can ride anything." Connor held a forkful of crab meat up to Dannie's mouth. "But I've got something better for you, Princess."

"Uncle Connor's a *true* knight."

"Aren't you Connor Ryan?" All five heads turned toward the bright-eyed blonde who'd suddenly appeared by the table. As she spoke, her face got steadily redder, her eyes even brighter. "Connor Ryan from Georgia Nights? You are, aren't you?"

Connor gave her an easy smile. "Yes, I am."

"Oh, I *love* your music. I saw you in L.A. You were wonderful! I can't believe I'm standing this close. Will you sign something for me?" She fumbled through the big macramé bag that hung from her shoulder.

Connor laughed. "Anything but a check, honey."

The girl glanced down at her restaurant bill and giggled. "Oh, no, not this. Here." She produced a small pad and a pen, which he accepted with a smile.

"Do me a favor?"

"Anything!"

Connor finished scrawling good wishes on the pad and handed it back to her, his engaging smile obviously turning her to putty. "Don't flash this around in here. Every tourist in the place will think he has to have one, too, even if he's never heard of Georgia Nights."

"Oh, I'm sorry." Bright red now, she clutched the pad to her breast and stammered, "You're eating...I wasn't thinking."

"No problem. It was nice meeting you." Connor's wink sent the girl off on a cloud.

"That was very smooth," Sarah noted.

"It doesn't happen often. When you're just one out of four, they don't usually recognize—"

"You're Connor Ryan, aren't you? I just heard that girl say..."

They left the restaurant with Dwight muttering something unflattering about teenagers, but the flash in Connor's eyes told Sarah that he'd enjoyed the recognition, probably all the more so because it irritated his father.

Connor negotiated the morning fog and traffic in a solemn mood. Roberta's parting comments had left a knot in his stomach, which he told himself was a sign of his old weaknesses. It was natural for his mother to refer to Dannie as Kevin's daughter. She *was* Kevin's daughter, though Connor himself had stopped thinking of her in those terms some time ago.

The knot was still there. What had really gotten to him was his mother's attitude toward Sarah. It was as though she expected Sarah to be Kevin's widow for the rest of her life when she hadn't even been Kevin's wife. "We want you to visit us often. We want Dannie to know who her father was, and, of course, we want to share our memories of him with you, too."

If they wanted to sit around fondling Kevin's memory, they could damn well do it without Connor around, and he could do without knots in his stomach.

"It's a good thing you aren't a family man, Connor."

"Why?"

"The Corvette suits you, but—" Sarah cast a pointed look behind her, where Dannie and the luggage seemed a bit crowded "—it's not built for kids."

"How do you like my car, Princess?"

"It's pretty," Dannie returned.

Connor's look was as pointed as Sarah's had been.

"If you had a beat-up '56 Mercury, she'd say it was pretty," Sarah protested.

"When we get home, we break out the Jeep. Practicality on wheels. It's the only thing I have that my father approves of."

"I'm surprised he doesn't have one of his own." Turning slightly in her seat, Sarah looked at him, choosing her words carefully. "It's hard to reconcile yourself to the fact that some of the people you're supposed to love are impossible to live with. You have a great deal of patience, Connor."

Remembering Sarah's errant brother, Connor smiled. The knot was gone. "Coming from someone whose name should be Patience, that's a nice compliment. Dad's not a bad guy, really. It's just that we're mismatched. We've never been able to please each other." He lifted one shoulder, never taking his eyes off the road. "It was different with Kevin."

"You and Kevin were two very different men," she observed. "Each likable in his own way."

"Kevin's way was *lovable*. How about mine?"

A coy brow angled upward. "I think that's a loaded question."

Connor pumped the Corvette a shot of gas and grinned with confidence. "I didn't expect an answer, either...not yet. I like to establish a firm foundation of *likable* and then ease on over to *lovable*."

"Is that your way?"

"That's...'m-y-y w-a-a-y.'" The singer's gesture to the windshield brought a giggle from Sarah. They had driven out of the fog and into the sunshine.

The view of the ocean from coast-hugging Highway 1 was not enough to keep Dannie from falling asleep in the back of the car. Sarah leaned back comfortably and enjoyed the ride through countryside that had everything—mountains and sea, orchards, pasture and towering trees. In keeping with his promise of redwoods, Connor headed inland, navigating the narrow, twisting mountain road through the jack-pine and madrone forest. Huge redwoods dwarfed the misty-silver Corvette as it wound its way deep in the forest of Big Basin State Park.

Connor parked the car near the round, log ranger station and gently shook Dannie awake. He laughed when her sleepy-eyed face brightened suddenly with her first glimpse of the trees around her. "Where are we?" she gasped. "Does a giant live here?"

"No, the Giant lives in another park." Connor pulled a soft suede jacket out of the car before shutting the door. "But Father of the Forest lives here, and so does the Mother Tree. Should we take a look?"

Dannie craned her neck to give Connor a quizzical look. Everything around her was up so high. "The trees have names?"

"They're special trees, so they have special names." As they walked, Connor drew Sarah next to him, his hand finding a comfortable hold at the base of her neck over the upturned collar of her lightweight jacket. "You girls warm enough?" he wondered. "It gets pretty cool down here in these woods."

She nodded, not because she was really warm enough, but because his hand felt so good where it was on her back, and it felt right to walk with him this way. It felt, for the moment, as though they belonged together, as though the little girl scampering up the path ahead belonged to both of them.

"This must be the forest primeval." Even the sound of her voice seemed small and insignificant. "It reminds me of a fairy-tale setting. *Hansel and Gretel* or something. Could we get lost?"

With half a smile, Connor teased, "Sure, if you want to."

"No, really."

"The trails are well marked," he said, "and I probably know them as well as any ranger. Trust me?"

"Of course." At his smile, she amended, "You don't have a gingerbread house at the end of the path, do you?"

His voice became an eerie whine. "Have I got sweets for you, my pretty!" Then he pulled her closer and whispered, "Sugar and spice and everything nice."

"That's what girls are made of," Sarah recited.

"I know. That's why I love to have them for dinner." He gave her a quick peck on the cheek and sang out with a rollicking cackle, which brought Dannie to heel.

"Uncle Connor, are you trying to scare us?"

"Of course not. I was just promising treats for later. See that, Princess?" He favored Sarah with a wink as he pointed to a large round burl growing out of the trunk near the base of one tree. "What does that look like to you?"

Dannie sized it up. "It looks like the tree is bouncing a beach ball."

Dannie's wide-eyed wonder was contagious. Connor felt it all anew as Sarah tipped her head back in amazement every few yards. He talked about the lumbering that was done in northern California in the last century, stripping acres of these ancient beauties, and of the successful replantings in some areas along with the struggle to save what was left of the prehistoric stands. Indeed, time seemed to stand still in this place, the sun's position in the sky becoming irrelevant in the depths of the forest. It was a private, quiet time, with only an occasional hiker to intrude.

Guiding them along the twig-and-needle carpet runner, Connor explained that there really were mother trees, whose young shoots grew around their root collars in "fairy circles," a term that delighted Dannie. Only the hardiest would survive, and eventually the mother tree would fall. That fact saddened her, but Connor explained quite matter-of-factly that it was nature's way. Within forty to sixty years, the mother's shoots could become two-hundred-foot redwood giants, and the forest would continue its timeless life cycle.

The drive to Connor's home continued through the redwood-blanketed Santa Cruz Mountains. Following the San Lorenzo River, they drove through another state park, bypassed the town of Santa Cruz and traveled several miles on a narrow back road before reaching Connor's secluded home overlooking the ocean. The house, a ranch-style rambler, was tucked into a hill, its sand-colored facade refusing to compete with the landscape to make a visual impression.

Though its style was completely different from her own home, Sarah loved the house from the moment she stepped into the red-quarry-tile foyer. There was a soft tranquillity here, and when she turned to Connor with her compliments on the tip of her tongue, she saw the calmness reflected in his face. Connor Ryan was home.

He was home, and he had Sarah and Dannie with him, and though he'd have to take a trip to Nashville in a few days, he was going to keep them here as long as he could. He needed to know what about them made him feel so good. Maybe he'd find a way to make it last.

"I'll show you Dannie's room first," he said, and with a suitcase in each hand he led the way past a sunken area with a gorgeous view of the ocean. Sarah turned her head all the way back over her shoulder as she followed, turning her attention to the hallway only after the view was completely behind her. "Great, huh?" Connor said. "That window and two others sold me on the house."

"Connor, Dannie and I can share a room. I have a feeling you've gone to...too...much...trouble... Connor!" The room's walls and carpeting were white, but everything else in it was pink—ruffled bedspread on the big brass bed, curtains, accents, stuffed panther.

"This looks suspiciously like a little girl's room." Sarah turned up an accusing brow. "Hardly your style."

First Class Romance

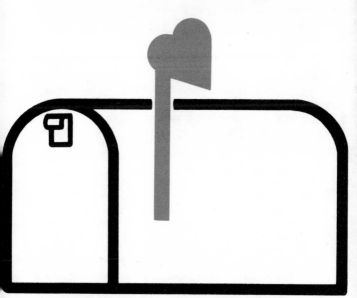

Delivered to your door by
Silhouette Special Edition®

Find romance at your door with 4 FREE novels from Silhouette Special Edition!

Slip away to a world that's as far away as your mailbox. A world of romance, where the pace of life is as gentle as a kiss, and as fast as the pounding of a lover's heartbeat. Wrap yourself in the special pleasure of having Silhouette Special Edition novels arrive at your home.

By filling out and mailing the attached postage-paid order card you'll receive—FREE—4 new Silhouette Special Edition novels (a $10.00 value) plus a FREE Folding Umbrella and Mystery Gift.

You'll also receive an extra bonus: our monthly Silhouette Books Newsletter. Then approximately every 4 weeks we'll send you six more Silhouette Special Edition novels to examine FREE for 15 days. If you decide to keep them, you'll pay just $11.70 (a $15.00 value) with no extra charge for home delivery and at no risk! You'll have the option to cancel at any time. Just drop us a note. Your first 4 books, Folding Umbrella and Mystery Gift are yours to keep in any case.

Silhouette Special Edition®

Mail this card today for

4 FREE BOOKS
(a $10.00 value)
and a Folding Umbrella and
Mystery Gift FREE!

Silhouette Special Edition®

Silhouette Books, 120 Brighton Rd., P.O. Box 5084, Clifton, NJ 07015-9956

☐ YES! Please send me my four Silhouette Special Edition novels FREE, along with my FREE Folding Umbrella and Mystery Gift, as explained in this insert. I understand that I am under no obligation to purchase any books.

NAME _____

(please print)

ADDRESS _____

CITY _____ STATE _____ ZIP _____

Terms and prices subject to change.
Your enrollment is subject to acceptance by Silhouette Books.

Silhouette Special Edition is a registered trademark.

CMS466

"That's what the decorator said. I think she thinks I'm getting kinky in my old age."

Sarah's jaw dropped. "You hired a *decorator*? You didn't even know I'd agree to come down here."

"*You* didn't know you'd agree to come down here," he corrected her, grinning a little sideways.

Sarah shook her head slowly as she surveyed the room. It was too sweet, too pretty and definitely too neat, but then no little girl had ever lived in it. "You hired a decorator," she repeated, "for a two- or three-day visit at most."

"I hope it'll get more use than that." He reached for Sarah's shoulders and turned her to face him. "This won't be the only time, Sarah. I care about . . . Dannie. I want to see her as often as I can."

"Is this my room, Uncle Connor?"

Together they looked down at the anxious little face. Sarah knew this was no time to discuss the logistics of an impossibly fragile relationship, and Connor took pleasure in answering the question. "I thought you might like to have two rooms—one on each side of the country."

"Like your uncle, who has two homes," Sarah muttered.

"I have an apartment in Nashville. This is my home." He gave Sarah a meaningful look. "This is my private life, Sarah. I bring few people here. For the most part, I'm a very private person, like you."

Sarah wanted to question his definition of terms. How did he measure "the most part," and how much privacy could there be for a man who was asked to sign autographs during dinner?

"Do you have a room for Mommy, too?"

"You haven't told me what you think of yours, Princess."

"Oh, I love it!" Connor bent down to receive the hug he saw coming. "But does it have a night-light?"

"Would I put you in a room without a night-light? It's in the base of that lamp." The lamp he indicated had a gracefully sculptured globe of pink glass. "And I do have a room for Mommy, too. She'll be relieved to know how little trouble I went to on her account." He cast Sarah an upward glance. "I changed the sheets."

"*You* changed the sheets?" Sarah wondered, a smile tickling the corners of her mouth.

"*Somebody* changed the sheets." Rolling to his feet, he lifted the bag he knew contained Sarah's clothes. "It's two doors down. Come on." As he passed the next door, he commented, "I'll be in this room, right next door, Princess. Your room has its own bathroom, but if you need anything, I'll know where to find it."

"She might need her mother," Sarah said quietly.

"I'll know where to find her, too." He pushed the last door open and set Sarah's bag inside. The touch of a button opened a bank of pale blue drapes, and there, again, was a view of the ocean. The entire room was cool blue, and Sarah recognized one of her paintings, *Girl by the Pond*, featured prominently on one wall.

"This looks suspiciously like a big boy's room," Sarah guessed. Connor shoved his hands in the pockets of his jacket and shrugged, looking very much the part of a little boy waiting for approval. Sarah was drawn to the window, and he followed. "Imagine having the Pacific Ocean sing you to sleep every night. How lovely! But it must be scary when it storms."

"You get used to it."

Sarah glanced around the room again and saw that Dannie was gone. "I don't want to take your bedroom, Connor, beautiful as it is. Please let me stay in the guest room."

The porcelain face she turned up to him was all softness—the innocent eyes of a fawn, her lower lip a tiny pink satin pillow. He saw himself laying his forehead, his eyelids, his mouth against that pillow, and he knew he wanted her in his bed even if he couldn't be there with her. He wanted to think of her sleeping where he'd slept.

"I've moved everything I need into the other room." He nodded toward the waves, now breaking gently before rolling in to wash the sand. "I see this view all the time. You enjoy it for a few days. If we get a storm—" he offered a slow grin "—we'll think of something."

"You'll have two of us to contend with."

"Sounds like fun." Putting an arm around her shoulders, he suggested, "Let me show you the rest of the house. What would you like for supper?"

"You do great omelets."

"I'm pretty good with steaks, too."

The center of the house was divided into three areas by single-step levels. The sunken living room was big enough to be impressive, small enough to be comfortable. Its style was light, airy and contemporary, its sandy colors warmed by muted red and brown tones. The kitchen was a step up from the living room, and the dining room, bright with skylights, was a level above that. Flanking the main rooms on the opposite side of the bedrooms was Connor's "play area." There was a den, a recreation room with weight machines, sauna and whirlpool, and finally, with another window to the sea, there was a music room. Sarah knew at once that it was a room for an artist's work. Another of her paintings hung here, and the third was in the living room.

"Nice little hideaway you've got here," Sarah remarked, following Connor into the kitchen. "How much time do you get to spend in it?"

"When I'm not on tour or recording, I'm here." Rummaging through the refrigerator, he found some milk. "Dannie probably needs something to eat right now. What does she like?"

"Peanut butter," Sarah announced, certain he wouldn't have it.

A single finger cocked in Sarah's direction registered the order, and a new jar was produced from the cupboard. "How about you? Peanut butter?"

"Nothing, thanks. So you come here to write your music?"

Connor turned to her, staring through her with disarming blue eyes. "I live here, Sarah. I'm not a Gypsy. I do all the things a person does in the place where he lives, and I also do my work here, my songwriting. This is not home base. This is *home*."

Again she wondered about definitions. Being here for a few months out of the year obviously made this home to him. "It's a beautiful place, Connor. A private paradise, perfect for an artist."

He smiled, wondering whether she could possibly mean herself. "Sure I can't interest you in any...peanut butter?"

The smile was returned. "I'm saving up for steak."

"Mommy! There's a TV in my room and a record player and..." Dannie pattered to a halt and eyed the jar in Connor's hand. She went from excited to sweet. "Can I have a peanut-butter sandwich, too, Uncle Connor?"

"Coming right up," he promised, putting a spin on the jar as he tossed it up in the air.

"You're determined to send me home with a spoiled brat," Sarah muttered.

Connor laughed, thinking better of telling her that he wasn't determined to send her home at all and he wasn't above spoiling Sarah herself.

Before supper, Connor showed Sarah and Dannie his horses—a pair of gray quarter-horse mares with rich black manes and tails. They were housed in a small barn tucked behind a stand of pines. Connor assured Dannie that they were taken care of even when he wasn't home, and he promised her a morning ride.

Connor's stretch of beach invited walking in the early twilight. Sarah bundled Dannie up against the chilly breeze, and the three followed the rocky path down the hill. Dannie asked Connor how to comb the beach, and then she held up a handful of seaweed. "Is this its hair? Mommy wouldn't let my hair get *this* tangled."

He led them to a cozy spot sheltered by the hill, where several heavy wooden deck chairs stood waiting in the sand. With Dannie in his lap, he insisted that Sarah join them in the same chair. Huddled together, they watched the waves shatter themselves against the long rock jetty and then limp peacefully to lap the shoreline with lolling tongues. Darkness came too quickly, but Connor promised more time with the ocean in the days to come.

Making supper was a joint project, with Connor grilling steaks outdoors while Sarah and Dannie worked on a magnificent salad and surprised him with a quick torte for dessert. When dessert came around, Dannie was losing in the struggle to keep her eyes open. By the time Connor had a fire going in the living room fireplace, Dannie was asleep in a chair. As before, Connor coveted the job of carrying the child to bed, but he left Sarah to get her settled in while he returned to the kitchen to resume his duties as host.

Sarah found him quite relaxed in front of the fire. In jeans and soft blue sweater, his flaxen hair burnished by the firelight, he looked the part of a young college boy, ready to impress his girl with all the proper amenities of romance. Sure enough, there was wine on the big stone hearth in front of him, ready to be poured into two waiting long-stemmed glasses. Sarah gave him a knowing smile. "I won't do the dishes myself, but I'll help," she offered, knowing it was not the activity he had in mind for them.

"They're done. What do you think this is, a busman's holiday?"

Laughter bubbling in her throat, Sarah dropped beside him on the expansive curve of the couch. "I think it's a plot," she said, "and I know I should be angry with you for it, but I'm too comfortable, and it's all been too nice."

"If you're enjoying yourself, then I confess to having plotted it." He poured two glasses of wine and offered in his eerie witch's voice, "Have a glass of mulberry wine, my dear. It will help you sleep."

She accepted. "*Mulberry* wine?"

"California rosé," he admitted with a shrug, "but what the hell?"

"The plot thickens." Lifting her glass in salute, she smiled, and he responded in kind.

"Dannie likes it here," Connor said, wondering immediately why he couldn't be more subtle.

"Of course she does. What's not to like? Sun, surf, trees, horses..."

"Me."

"You especially. You aren't what I would have expected from...someone like you."

"What's *someone like me*?" Shifting into a Southern drawl, he protested, "I'm just a plain country boy, honey. I do a little pickin' an' singin', is all." She rolled her eyes and groaned, but his open-handed gesture asked her to reconsider. "Hey, listen, it's perfectly possible for someone you know to suddenly become someone everybody knows about. With us it just happened in reverse. Now you know I'm human."

"Just a regular guy." Over the rim of her glass, she cast him a look of doubt. "Who has teenagers hounding him in restaurants for autographs."

"They like what I do."

"They also like the way you look, the way you..."

He shrugged all that off. "Whatever. They don't like *me*. They don't know me. They know what they read, which is a bunch of fairy tales."

She set her glass down and found herself leaning closer to him. "They know your music, and that's part of you, Connor. I guess I assumed the lyrics to pop music were just part of the act, but since I met you, I've been listening. It's more than lyrics, it's..."

"Part of the act? Are your colors part of your act?"

"They're part of my vision, just as your lyrics, your composition are part of yours. The people who know your music know a great deal about you, Connor." The hand she laid on his shoulder was meant to be reassuring, but it became a two-way conductor of a charge that simultaneously pulsed through both bodies.

"Then it follows that—" his mouth had gone dry, and he had to swallow "—someone who's attracted to your paintings would be attracted to you, too."

Suddenly she was in his arms, meeting his kiss with the full measure of her need. Her tongue danced with his, wanting him, welcoming him, celebrating his desire for her. She wanted his passion, knowing instinctively that it would be tempered by his gentle nature. There was nothing to fear from this man...unless it was the fear of loving him.

He touched his lips to her eyelids, her temple, the softest part of her neck. She was the softness, the serenity he needed in his life, and he wanted to bury himself in that now, to burrow in it, to cover himself with softness. Softness must be handled with great care, he told himself, and he tasted the pearlized shell of her ear with the tip of his tongue. The shiver that ran through her then was absorbed into his own body, and he wanted more.

He lifted her sweater by quarter inches, easing her down on the couch as he kissed each piece of skin he exposed. The front clasp on her bra came open quickly. His hands slowed to let his eyes feast first. She was small and firm and lovely, and her pink nipples were tight with anticipation. The grip she had on his shoulders and the bright excitement in her eyes said, *yes,* said, *kiss them, too, Connor.* And he did. She sighed his name and laced her fingers in his hair to keep him close. He made her throb for him, and he knew the throbbing, too.

"Only if it's what you want, Sarah," he whispered, then traced an aureole with his tongue to be sure she could want nothing else.

"Oh, Connor..."

"I would never hurt you," he promised. "I'll give you everything you need. Just tell me..."

"I can't." He froze for a moment, then raised his head to look into her face. Her eyes were bright with both pleasure and fear, and he felt his throat tighten. "Not yet." She caught his face between her hands and searched his eyes for the patience he'd shown so many times before. "I'm not impetuous anymore, Connor."

On a ragged sigh, he dropped his head to her chest, gathering her in his arms.

"Forgive me," she whispered.

His mind spun with the crazy thought that he would like nothing more than to make love, here and now. He knew it was unfair of him not to take her wants into consideration but it was part of a feeling he had for her. There was nothing fair about feelings.

"I was going to ask the same of you," he said. "I wasn't thinking. I wanted to make love to you."

"I . . . wanted to make love to you, too."

They held each other in silence then, sharing both disappointment for the present moment and promise for the times to come.

Chapter Seven

Having lain awake all night, Connor had mentally mapped every inch of the dim ceiling above him. He wondered what kind of nightgown Sarah wore. He pictured her in white silk, her mink-colored hair spilling over his blue pillows. In his mind she slept peacefully, dreaming of him.

The clock told him it was technically too early to get up, but it was certainly too late to go to sleep. Today's activities would start early, anyway. Morning was the best time for tide pools. Dressing in jeans and a fisherman-knit sweater, Connor crept into Dannie's room. She looked too pretty to disturb, but he knew if he started with Sarah, he'd be tempted to crawl in bed beside her.

When he sat beside Dannie on the bed, she curled toward him and shoved a thumb in her mouth without waking. He watched instinct at work as she sucked vigorously, and it struck him that, as little experience as he'd had with small children, there must be some instincts at work in him, too. He would love this child as fiercely as any natural father could.

"Are we going to ride horses today, Uncle Connor?" Like everything else about Dannie, her yawn was contagious.

"Among other things. I've got plans, kid, big plans. We don't want to waste a minute." Poking through her suitcase, he found what seemed close to a small version of what he was wearing.

When he handed her the clothes, she shielded her flat chest with the flannel nightgown she'd just taken off. Lips pursed, her blue eyes flashed him a harbinger of the proper lady she would one day be. "Turn around, Uncle Connor. I can get myself dressed."

"Excuse me," he said with a serious nod, and turned away smiling. With his back to her, he launched into the agenda for the day. They'd explore parks and beaches, stroll the boardwalk and check out the shops in Santa Cruz, and, as promised, they'd ride the horses.

"Isn't today Saturday?" Dannie asked.

"It sure is."

"I'll miss cartoons." She gave that some seconds of consideration. "But I don't care. You can turn around now, Uncle Connor. Would you tie my shoes?"

Dannie was assigned to awaken her mother while Connor whipped up some scrambled eggs and coffee, but when she was certain Sarah was getting out of bed, she dashed back to the kitchen, where things were already happening. Gliding on crepe soles, Sarah followed her nose to the kitchen area, but she stopped before she was noticed and stood back for a moment, swallowing at the prickling in her throat. With Connor's close direction, Dannie was setting the table while he poured coffee.

She'd never associated masculine with domestic, nor handsome with patient and selfless. A child can be perfectly well adjusted with only her mother to rear her, Sarah reminded herself. Yet there was something lovely about this moment of closeness between the man and the child. Sarah hesitated to intrude. A woman can have her own life, her child and her career and be perfectly content without a man, she reminded herself again. Yet there was a heady sweetness about having this man around, and the scene at the table beckoned her to savor that sweetness.

"Look, Mommy, we made breakfast. Uncle Connor says we need a good breakfast this morning."

"Oh?" Sarah accepted a steaming mug of coffee from Connor's hand. "Are we planning something strenuous?"

"We're planning lots of things," Dannie reported, obviously pleased with her role as planner's assistant.

"Long day ahead, ladies. Eat hearty. Oh, did I say good morning yet?" Leaning across the chair that stood between them, Connor slipped a hand behind Sarah's neck and gave her a quick kiss. "Hope you got a good night's sleep."

With a look, she told him she'd had the same sort of night he'd had. He smiled, gratified.

"Uncle Connor, that's the same way you kissed me this morning. You're supposed to give Mommy the big-girl kiss." Dannie folded her arms in expectation.

"The kid's got a good point." The longer kiss was warm morning sunshine, a welcome to today. "Good morning," he repeated softly.

"It is a good morning," she agreed, wondering at the fluttering in her stomach. "Thanks for the coffee. Anything left for me to do?"

"Eat."

Sarah filled her nose with the aroma once more and took a chair. "That I can handle. From the smell of it, I'd say you two are pretty good cooks."

"We make a great team." Connor tossed Dannie a partner's wink.

Natural Bridges State Park was one of Connor's favorite spots. The drive took them past the eroded rock arches that gave the park its name. At Sarah's request, they stopped while she made a quick sketch of a congregation of gulls and cormorants that were using one arch as a base. Then Connor parked the car and led them to a high area of the rocky beach. Sarah settled in to sketch, while Connor and Dannie poked around from tide pool to tide pool, the man squatting on his haunches almost as the child did and exhibiting no less fascination.

In the bright light of morning, Sarah watched at a distance for a while. This was Dannie at her best. She never tired of watching ants or following butterflies, though the activity often tried Sarah's patience, as undoubtedly it would Connor's. But Sarah continued to sketch, and her companions continued to poke, both heads glinting gold in the sun as they bent together over some tiny find. Connor's interest, apparently genuine, showed no signs of flagging, and Sarah realized that Dannie wasn't running to her with every little discovery. Finally, Sarah tucked her sketch pad under her arm and decided to see what they had under such close scrutiny.

"Look, Mommy! Periwinkles!" Dannie pointed to a cluster of small snails clinging to a rock. Tugging at Sarah's hand, she dragged her back a few steps. "And here's a black turban snail. Uncle Connor, he came out again. Oh-oh, there he goes, back in his shell. We scared him." Dannie dug down deep in her jacket and came up with a small shell, which she held out to Sarah on a chubby palm. "This is a hermit crab inside here. Uncle Connor says I can only hold him for a little while, but I have to leave him. We can only keep shells that nobody lives in, and we can't take the ones on this beach because the hermit crabs need them."

Dannie's eyes were bright with excitement, and Connor's, certainly bigger, were even brighter, if that was possible. Negotiating the rocks with the agile grace of a tightrope walker, he motioned to them. "Over here! I found a bigger crab."

He gave Sarah a hand up to his perch on a small ledge, but Dannie scrambled up beside him on her own. Rolling back a small rock, he exposed a small clawed creature that reared up indignantly, brandishing pinchers in a demand to be left alone. Connor identified it as a lined shore crab. He had names for all the seaweed, too—sea palms, sea lettuce, surf grass.

"How would you like to wear this one in the boudoir?" he asked Sarah, swinging a long piece of wet weed in her direction. "It's a feather boa."

"Perhaps if I were a mermaid," she suggested gaily, acting out her fantasy as she told it. "I'd lunch on sea lettuce and lie in the surf grass, my feather boa flung about my neck for a touch of glamour."

"If you were a mermaid, I think I wouldn't mind being a sailor or a fisherman."

"My shoreline crabs would pinch you if you tried to catch me," she warned, and punctuated the word with a playful pinch on his thigh.

The gesture stimulated him unexpectedly, and the flash in his eyes became a flashing smile. He grabbed her wrist and twisted her arm behind her back, throwing an arm across the front of her shoulders to immobilize her against him. "They're *lined shore* crabs, and I think I'd like that," he growled in her ear. "Wanna try it again?"

Sarah giggled, shaking her head.

"What should I do with her, Princess? She's upsetting all the wildlife."

Dannie liked seeing her mommy play with Uncle Connor. When they laughed together, it made her want to laugh, too, even if she didn't know what they were laughing about. "Maybe you should send her to bed without supper."

"Don't you think she deserves a spanking?"

From her perch several yards from the wrestling match, Dannie shook her head. "Not unless she just won't stop being bad."

"So that's how it works," he called out, and then in Sarah's ear he whispered, "I'll let you go if you promise not to stop being bad."

"Oh!" she squealed as he gave her a warning squeeze. His play delighted her, but she knew how readily her skin bruised. "I promise!"

Their trek brought them to a sandier area where there were fewer live specimens to watch, but they found sand dollars, which Connor said could be taken home. Before leaving the park he took them to a grove of eucalyptus trees, where clusters of orange-and-black monarch butterflies hung from the branches. Connor explained that they were still tired from their October migration of three thousand miles and wished that Dannie and Sarah had been there for Welcome Back Monarchs Day.

The beautiful weather brought a good crowd out to the Santa Cruz boardwalk, which was open only on weekends in the off-season. Sarah agreed to ride in the bumper cars, and she found the old carousel with its classic wooden horses and calliope music irresistible. But she stood on the ground and watched in sympathetic terror as Connor and Dannie arced high over the crowd in their swaying ferris-wheel chair.

They ate lunch by a view of the harbor and then strolled the Pacific Avenue Garden Mall downtown. After shopping for the few items she needed, Sarah enjoyed browsing through small specialty stores. Dannie found a jumpsuit with appliquéd dolphins that reminded her of her "pink-elephant pants," and Connor insisted that since Uncle Jerry had bought the elephant pants, Uncle Connor would buy the dolphin pants. He also bought a conch shell that caught Dannie's fancy and a glass horse and a stuffed crab. Sarah realized after the fourth gift that protesting his extravagance was useless.

A group of street musicians was drawing a crowd in front of an antique shop, and Connor and Sarah joined the crowd at Dannie's request. Between songs, one bearded guitarist came over to Connor and offered a handshake.

"How's it going, man?"

"Real smooth, Randy," Connor responded, and nodded toward the group. "You've got a good sound here. What are you doing with it?"

"Playing some of the old spots. Sit in on one with us?" Connor accepted the proffered guitar, looping the strap over his head and testing out the strings with a chord. "Take the lead on 'Misty River Morning,'" Randy urged.

Connor glanced at the crowd. It looked small and harmless. There were so many copyists these days that he could usually get away with pretending to be one of them. He glanced back at his old friend and smiled. "Just one."

The group swung into the song as though they'd practiced it together, but Connor carried it. With his voice he carried it to the crowd, offering it for their pleasure just as he did for any paying audience. With his eyes, he carried it to Sarah, laid it in her lap like a treasured gift. It touched her soul and filled her eyes with shimmery gratitude.

It's a misty river morning, babe
The world's just gettin' out of bed
You lie sleepin' soft beside a happy man
Whose mind's on all the sweet, sweet love
we made.

That's how it would be with this man, Sarah thought.
He was a man who longed to give, and his lovemaking
would be a gift—gentle as his song promised. Her skin
felt tight from head to foot, and her whole body became a pulse point as she listened to the last words of
the song. *You and me and the river, babe, makin' misty*
morning love.

He left them stunned. Then he had them clapping,
pitching handfuls of change and bills into an open guitar case, and the hazy spell was broken.

"Sure sounds like the record to me," one young man
declared. "You oughta try out for Georgia Nights, fella.
You're every bit as good as any of them."

"Thanks," Connor said with a nod toward the voice
in the crowd. "Would you put that in writing? I'll take
it with me when I take the bus to Nashville."

"Sure thing," the voice promised on the end of a
good-natured laugh.

Randy thanked Connor with a hearty handshake and
a slap on the back. Each musician took his turn shaking Connor's hand and wishing him well. The man in
the crowd hung back, watching the proceedings and
asking finally, "Hey, man, you really going to Nashville?"

"Sure am," Connor said.

The man stuck out a hand. "Hey, good luck. I wasn't kidding. In fact, I think you're even *better* than the record. You're gonna do great, man, just great."

"I hope so. Thanks for the encouragement. It's really a long shot, but what the hell, right?"

"Right. Go for it, man. I'm telling you, you could be with Georgia Nights. I'm a big fan of theirs. You go for it." With a wave and another nod of reassurance, the man took his leave.

Connor and his friends enjoyed the moment when the man was out of earshot, but Connor's parting advice echoed his young fan's. "You guys are good. You go for it!"

"Did you know them?" Sarah asked as they walked along.

"Randy and I used to be part of a group a few years back."

"You were a street musician, too, then?"

"I've played my music in the street, in back-street bars, high-school gyms, you name it."

"Randy's good," Sarah observed. "Why is he still playing street corners?"

Connor shoved his hands in his pockets and shrugged. "He wasn't willing to take too many risks. He doesn't do too badly here, and at least he knows what he's got."

Sarah could understand that. Of the myriad people who dreamed of fame, there were probably many who had the talent, but only a few were really cut out to endure the rocky road that must be traveled. "Why did you take the risks?" she wondered.

"I had nothing to lose." He caught her arm and pointed to a building claiming to be the Artists' Co-op. "You'll enjoy this place," he promised, changing the focus of conversation.

"I thought you said this wasn't a busman's holiday."

"Can you walk on by?" he challenged.

Sarah grinned. "Of course not."

Crafts for sale at the co-op were of admirable quality, and Sarah examined pieces of handmade glassware and pottery that struck her fancy. She particularly liked a small wood carving, a child with a duck, that reminded her of the quality she'd seen in Munich. Connor stood to the side with Dannie, who saw little that interested her. But Connor took quiet consideration of everything Sarah touched, every comment she made, anything that reflected her taste. He watched while a weaver persuaded Sarah to try a handmade serape, woven in shades of emerald and white that looked lovely with Sarah's coloring. She wouldn't buy it for herself, of course.

They stopped for a late lunch at a sidewalk café, and while Sarah and Dannie munched on batter-fried shrimp and listened to a swinging jazz band, Connor excused himself for a few moments. It wasn't long before he was threading his way back among the strollers at an easy jog, a package under his arm.

"Where did you go?" Sarah wondered, eyeing the package.

Connor dropped into a chair and hoisted his soft drink for a healthy swallow. "Went back to the co-op.

I asked them to send all the things you suggested out to the house.''

"All the things *I* suggested?''

"Yeah, the stuff you liked—the pots, that glass gull, the wood carving—everything you picked out for me.''

Aghast, Sarah sputtered, "Picked out for...Connor, I didn't...those things were...''

"They were great, every one of them.'' He leaned toward her with a conspiratory grin. "That decorator's a nice enough lady, but she makes the place feel uncomfortable. The furniture's okay, but she comes up with the most awful...art pieces, she calls them. I like your stuff. I like what you picked out today.''

"I didn't suggest that you *buy* them,'' Sarah insisted, her eyes still wide with disbelief.

"The things you said were good...they really *were* good, weren't they?''

"Of course.''

He craned his neck to give her an unexpected peck on the cheek. "I knew you wouldn't let me down.''

"You could have picked them out yourself if that's the kind of thing you like.''

"There was too much stuff in there. You went right to certain things, and each time I said to myself, 'Hey, yeah, that's the one.''' He laughed at himself and chomped on a cold shrimp. "I'm the guy who put horse feed in a handmade pot. Now I've got it sitting in the living room filled with cattails and marsh grasses. Looks pretty good.''

"I noticed,'' Sarah said, remembering. "Scotch has a nice touch with clay.''

Connor felt a twinge of jealousy, and he decided then and there he was going to show her what a nice touch *he* had. Catching himself, he smiled, telling himself he meant *artistic* touch, as in keyboard, synthesizer, songwriting... not in getting his hands on the soft body he longed to touch.

"What are you smiling about?" Sarah wondered.

On a chuckle, Connor chose his response. "Scotch. He must've ground his back teeth when he saw that pot full of horse feed. Can't blame him, either. Oh, here." He reached for the package as though he'd just remembered it, though that wasn't the case. He'd been anxious to give it to her. "This is something no one but you should wear."

Sarah took the package and unwrapped it carefully, knowing full well what it was and trying to decide whether to let her excitement show. On the fringe of her awareness, she heard Dannie's comments approving of the fact that Mommy was getting a present and Connor's response that Mommy deserved one, since Dannie had gotten so many. Sarah held up the serape. "Connor..."

"I know the weaver isn't a personal friend of yours like the guy who made your skirt, but still... it looks great on you, Sarah."

She clutched it to her and smiled at him. There was no point in protesting the cost of it. She wanted it, and he knew that. "The weaver is a friend now," she said. "And so are you. Thank you, Connor."

She'd accepted without protest. He was amazed, and when he spoke, he found a strange hoarseness in his voice. "It...the colors seem right...with your hair and eyes."

"How did you know that the person who made my skirt was a guy?" she wondered.

"Just a hunch," he returned with a shrug.

"Just a friend," she found herself telling him. "A fellow artist."

"Like me?"

"No. Not like you." With her eyes she told him that there was no one like him.

By the time they returned home, Connor's purchases had arrived, and Sarah enjoyed the role of adviser as they decided where each piece should go. Trying one piece of pottery out on a high shelf, Sarah discovered dust, and she informed Connor that his housekeeper was overpaid.

He imagined telling that to fiery-eyed Carmel and laughed. "Scratch one decorator and one housekeeper. You wouldn't be looking for a job, would you?" Hands at her waist, he lifted her down from a small step stool. "I could fly you out, say, twice a month?"

Sliding her hands from his shoulders to his chest, she waited to be released. "That's a long time between cleanings. What will you do in the meantime?"

"Languish in my own clutter."

They stood that way for a moment, touching only with arms and hands. It was like lingering to enjoy the aroma of a pie fresh from the oven and still too hot to eat. Even the anticipation felt good.

"Your niece is waiting for her horseback ride," Sarah reminded him. "If you don't keep your promise, you'll witness tiny-tot rebellion, and your image of her will be shattered.''

''I intend to keep all my promises.'' He held her gaze for a moment before asking, ''Shall we saddle up and catch the last of the daylight?''

''I have a feeling I'm going to be sore tomorrow.''

''Then we'll stay home tomorrow,'' he promised quietly into her hair. ''And I'll minister to all your needs.''

A shiver ran the length and breadth of Sarah's body—invisibly, she hoped. She was not a blushing maiden, and yet she felt seven kinds of anxiety all at once. Turning out of his arms without raising her eyes to meet his, she muttered something about getting Dannie ready for her ride.

A totally romantic notion prodded Sarah to wear her new serape. She laughed at the image she conjured of herself riding barefoot, a colorful gathered skirt billowing against her legs, hair flying in the wind as she galloped over the hills carrying a message for Zapata. Really, Sarah, she thought. You with all the courage of a mouse. She wore her most practical shoes, but she did leave her hair unbound.

Connor watched Sarah mount the gentler of the two mares and settle herself in the western saddle. Satisfied that she knew what she was doing, he put Dannie in his saddle and hoisted himself up behind her. When he figured everyone was broken in at a walk, he picked up the pace. Dannie giggled as she bobbled in front of him, but Sarah's horse was smooth gaited, and she sat the trot without difficulty. On a stretch of white beach he let Sarah lead them in an easy canter, and he pulled off to her side, the better to watch her serape flutter in the breeze and her dark hair ripple behind her. Her porcelain beauty was no fantasy. Connor conjured nothing but the prospect of having her in his arms.

But it wasn't as easy as he'd thought. When Dannie was sleeping contentedly in her bed, and the woman he'd wanted since the first moment he'd seen her was seated beside him in front of a crackling fire, he couldn't think of one glib line. He sat there for what felt like an eternity, staring into the fire, not completely comfortable with the slow burn he had going in the pit of his stomach. She probably thought he was some kind of tomcat on the prowl.

Sarah supposed he didn't find her much different from any other female groupie. Maybe she'd taken a little longer than most, but by the size of the tight wad of nerves in her stomach, she knew he'd worked his magic on her. She'd stopped kidding herself about having any resistance to him whenever he touched her, and she told herself to be realistic about what this was— a brief romantic encounter with a man whose world was much too big for her. *Right now, the thing to do is not ask yourself to accept that. Leave that for later, when it's too late.*

"Did you notice the way Dannie was walking after we took that ride?" Sarah asked, tentatively breaking the silence.

"Cute little swagger on her, wasn't it?" Connor's chuckle faded into another few moments of silence, and then he took his turn. "Can I get you anything? A glass of wine?"

Sarah shook her head. "No, thanks. I'm fine."

You're fine? You look as nervous as I feel. "Tell me about your parents," he suggested quickly, and at her skeptical glance he added, "or... or anything else you feel like talking about."

Their eyes met again, and they both laughed. It seemed natural to reach for her hand, and so he did. The contact brought them both a sigh of relief.

"My mother was a very hardworking lady who hoped that her son would become a successful businessman and her daughter would find a good husband. We both disappointed her, but she never complained. She died a little more than three years ago. Dannie doesn't remember her at all."

"But you haven't stopped missing her," Connor offered quietly. Sarah shook her head. "And your father?"

"He left my mother in pursuit of his theatrical dreams. He's a television actor of sorts." The bitterness was in her voice, much as she tried to deny it in her mind.

"Of sorts?"

"Well, he's been in a lot of soap operas. They usually kill him off within a year. Once in a while he'll show up in a commercial, and then he'll get another soap." She hastened to add, "Of course, I never watch them myself."

"You don't have time." He gave her a knowing look.

"Well... once in a while."

"Once in a while when you want to get a glimpse of your dad. He never came around much after he split with your mom?"

"He never came around at all, which is just as well. His influence might have made Jerry worse than he is."

"One of those crazy theatrical people, huh?" She nodded without looking up at him. "Kind of footloose and fancy-free? Totally unreliable?"

"I'm sure they're not *all*..." She met his gaze now, and he saw the fear just before she masked it with what she considered to be a mature outlook. "I'm sure they're not all that way. My mother simply married the wrong man. She was the first to admit it."

"Do you think they'll ever come up with a new kind of divorce?" Connor wondered. "A kid realizes things just aren't working out, and he says, 'I got the wrong father. I'm going to divorce him and look for a more suitable one.'"

"Would you divorce yours?"

He thought about it and shook his head, finally voicing his "No." And then he laughed at the news he'd just handed himself. "I'd go right on hoping for things to change. You?"

She thought if understanding were a color, it would be the blue of his eyes. "The same, I guess."

"Of course the same, Sarah Benedict. You're loyal. All he gave you was his name, but you've got a stockpile of love for him, though it's all hardened over with a shell of disappointment." He cupped his free hand around her cheek, almost beseechingly. "I could put some of that loyalty to good use, Sarah Benedict. Have you got any you could spare for another crazy theatrical person?"

She closed her eyes, summoning strength. Could she parcel it out in small doses? Was it possible for her to give a man one or two nights' worth of loyalty, just a small piece of her heart? She'd gone so long without giving any, and she wanted to give, longed to give to *this* man.

Her silence was his answer. He drew away from her. "I have some work to do," he announced in a stranger's voice. "You're probably very tired."

When Sarah opened her eyes, he was gone.

He did, indeed, have work to do. He had to earn her trust. After two cigarettes, he toyed with some lyrics he'd been working on, synthesized some background, experimented with some chord progressions on the guitar and finally decided he'd worn himself out. He could probably fall asleep. Well, maybe after a glass of wine. He'd take the tomcat in him, the theatrical crazy person and the new part, which was behaving suspiciously like a lovesick calf, and he'd anesthetize them all with a glass of good wine before putting them to bed.

He felt pretty confident after half a glass. Everything was cool. All systems were shutting down nicely. But when he headed down the hall, he realized that he'd forgotten to address one stubborn aspect of his nature. The latent rebel. The damned nuisance walked him right past the guest room and tapped at his own bedroom door. True to form, when the misty white vision appeared at the door, the rebel had nothing to say. He just stood there, waiting.

Sarah tried without success to swallow the pulsing in her throat. She took his hand, letting him know that her silence hadn't been a refusal. He closed the door behind him and took her in his arms, his mouth finding hers on instinct. His hand slid tightly along the length of her back and took firm hold of her buttocks, pulling her against his body so there could be no mistaking what he wanted. She whimpered and drew his tongue deeper into her mouth in acceptance. His heart soared. He filled both hands with her and pressed her tighter, rotating against her until she was breathless.

He took her to his bed and lay her against the cool sheets. The blue room was moonlit, and her face was the color of a blue-white star. Strong arms propped him above her, bent for a kiss, straightened for another look and then bent to allow him to dip his head again.

"I need you, Sarah," he confessed against her temple.

"I wanted you to come to me, Connor. I willed it."

"I came because I couldn't *not* come. I wanted to give you more time...all you needed...but I don't know how much time you'll give me."

She locked her hands behind his neck and pulled his ear to her mouth, whispering. "What I have to give you has nothing to do with time." Her tongue traced the curve of his ear, and he shivered. She pushed his sweater up and pulled handfuls of shirttail free from his pants while he breathed a line of kisses along the plunge her nightgown took to her breasts. Lacking patience with it, he peeled his sweater over his head, and she helped him undo the buttons on his shirt so that she could touch the pads of muscle over his chest.

His eager mouth found those small firm breasts and nuzzled them beneath the silky fabric before nosing her nightgown aside for a taste of nourishing sweetness. Her nipple was a firm berry in his mouth, and he was a hungry man, but he would only nibble excruciatingly gently, until she writhed and arched beneath him.

"I've only just started, sweet Sarah," he whispered, his breath hot against her breast. "This is only the beginning."

He was quick to remove the rest of his clothes but, oh, so slow to remove hers. He wanted to kiss and touch and taste each inch as he uncovered her. Her skin grew tight, and the blood flowed through her body like fire, pooling and pulsating beneath the parts of her skin his hands found most enticing.

"Connor, Connor, your hands are heavenly torture."

"I want to know you, love. I learn best by touch." He nipped at the hollow under her pelvic bone. "I have to take what I want to learn in my hands, roll it between my fingers, discover its texture." He dipped his tongue into the hollow of her navel, and she shuddered. "I remember by taste and by touch and by smell. I'm very primitive that way."

"Do you always…learn with such…agonizingly slow deliberation?" she panted.

"Yes," he groaned, his hand finding the hot, moist place he wanted for his own. "I'm a slow learner." He felt her hands clutch his hair, and he moved to taunt her breast while his hand worked elevating magic. When she shuddered against him uncontrollably, he soothed her, holding her close, and whispered, "But once I learn something, it's mine. It belongs to all my senses, and it never gets away from me. Are you prepared for that, Sarah? Are you ready for me?"

Her own hand fluttered and found him, touched him and drew him home. "Come learn one more part of me," she entreated. "This is the deeper part of me, the part that will make you mine."

Driving deeply, he knew he'd found his perfect fit, the piece of life's puzzle that he'd been cut to match.

Chapter Eight

There was little sleeping in Connor's big bed that night, but there was much learning. Indeed, Sarah found Connor's method to be very effective, and she put it to practice on him. They dozed in each other's arms, but Connor woke just as the sky began to lighten. He shifted slightly, and Sarah stirred with a soft, pleasured moan.

"Here comes the morning, Sarah."

His voice caressed her half-conscious brain, and she saw him bringing her the sun in a chariot just before she opened her eyes to his sleepy smile. "Did you bring it with you?" she asked.

"What?"

"The morning." She snuggled against his chest and closed her eyes again. "You brought me everything else I needed."

He chuckled. "Are you angling for breakfast in bed, sweet Sarah?"

"Mmm. I think there's a toll-free number you can call."

"Really? Got it handy?"

"I think you have to give them twenty-four hours' notice."

"What good is that? How do you know you're going to want breakfast in bed twenty-four hours ahead of time?" Cradling her in one arm, he leaned forward to shift several pillows behind them. "Scoot up just a little," he instructed. "The show's about to start."

They cuddled, kissing each other wherever was handy, but when the horizon reddened, they gave it their full attention. The gold fireball rose from the ocean's depths like the eye of God, letting there be light across the waters, splashing up on the beach and streaming through Connor Ryan's bedroom window. "So you found each other," it seemed to say. "That's good."

"Oh, Connor..." Sarah breathed, throwing back the covers and moving toward the huge window as though magnetized. "Connor, look how beautiful...*feel* how beautiful." Connor followed, but he stood by the foot of the bed, watching.

Naked, she stood before the sun, raising her arms above her head and stretching on her toes. She was Venus, closer to the sun than anything earthly, and the light painted the front of her body gold in celebration.

Connor was awed, afraid to touch her, struck for an instant by the notion that if he did, he would burst into flame. When she turned to him and held out both her hands, he couldn't move. Then she smiled, and she was Sarah again. He took her hands in his, shaking his head at his foolishness.

"I must look a sight," she said with a laugh, "but I don't care."

"You're a lovely sight, and I *do* care. What's this?" He released her left arm as he drew her other arm closer, gingerly touching the marks he'd found on its soft underside. "What happened here?"

"You twisted my arm, remember?" she said lightly. "It's not . . ."

"But I was just playing," he protested, his eyes wide with disbelief. "I couldn't have . . ."

"It's nothing," she assured him. "I bruise too easily."

"But I must've hurt you."

"Not at all. I often get bruises without even knowing where they came from." He was still staring at her arm, mortified. "Really," she offered with conviction.

"Did I hurt you last night when I . . ."

"No." His eyes met hers, and she shook her head. Still, he dipped his head to touch his lips to the pale purple mark on her arm, and something tugged at her heart. Winding her arms around his neck, she stepped between his feet and held herself close to him. "You could never hurt me, gentle Connor. Last night . . . you gave me something I've never had before."

"You mean . . . never? Not even with . . ."

Dropping her head back, she lay one finger over his lips, shaking her head. "Never. Not with anyone else."

He tightened his arms around her, wishing he could surround her with a wall of himself. "Then I'm your first lover, my sweet Sarah."

"Yes, you are," she whispered against his shoulder, and her voice constricted around the bittersweet note of it.

"I'll be a good one. Always. I promise. I'll never leave you wanting." He ran the heel of his hand down the length of her spine and then massaged her with the circular movement of his palms. "I'll never bruise you again."

"Don't promise that," she pleaded. "You'd have to wrap me in cotton, which would leave me wanting."

"I want to wrap you in me, and myself in you. You know what happens when you rub up against me like this in an undressed state?" He pressed her hips into his.

"Umm, yes, I think I get your point."

"I think you're about to," he growled, lowering her to the carpet.

"Connor, the door..."

"Locked," he breathed over her breast.

"But..."

"It's all right," he assured her. "It's very... very...early. This is our time, Sarah."

"Oh..."

"That's right, sweet Sarah. Want me."

"I do."

"Tell me."

"I want you, Connor. I want...Connor. Oh, Connor, yes."

"You have Connor, Sarah," he whispered, rocking slowly inside her. "Be good to him. He'll never leave you wanting."

They couldn't keep this up much longer, Sarah realized, giving the arm that cushioned her head a parting kiss. "This is where I tear myself away and head for the shower," she announced. "And where you split the scene altogether."

"In the altogether?" He reached for her ankle, but missed as she skipped out of reach.

"In your pants, mister." They landed across his legs, followed by his shirt and sweater.

"Thrown out of my own bedroom," he groaned.

"These arrangements were your idea," she reminded him, and just before she closed the bathroom door, she tossed, "See you at breakfast," over her shoulder.

Many moments later, Sarah stepped from the shower, her head wrapped in a towel, and was handed a cup of coffee. She frowned, setting the mug aside. "Breakfast in the bathroom?"

"Just coffee." He mounted two tiled steps, set his own mug down and lifted a large round lid, which Sarah had already mentally dubbed King Kong's privy, having no idea what else it could be. At the flip of a switch, something in the privy started whirling. "But you might want breakfast here, too, once you get used to it."

"We can't keep the door locked all morning."

"Here." He tossed her her swimming suit, and she noticed, at second glance, that he wore one, too, though it was a rather skimpy model. "Dannie's still sound asleep, but I've left the door unlocked."

"We're going swimming in the bathtub?"

"Hot tub, my pretty little pilgrim."

Still wet from the shower, Sarah squirmed into her suit and stepped up to the platform to peer into the tub. "Cauldron, more like," she judged.

Connor laughed. "Nothing of the sort, my dear. It's just a pot of soup. Test it with your sweet little finger, and tell me whether it's hot yet."

Picking up her end of the game, she narrowed her eyes at him. "I get it. You can't test it yourself because water will melt the likes of you." Dipping her foot into the bubbling water, she kicked him a spray. "Take that!"

"Ungrateful wench!" he cried. "I'll teach you." He reached for her arms, but she held her hands up in surrender.

"At the risk of getting any more bruises, I'll go peacefully." She lowered herself into the water, and Connor retrieved her coffee and followed her.

"I forgot. A *real* princess gets bruised by a pea twenty mattresses beneath her."

"I think you've read all my favorite fairy tales."

"My brother...my *mother* read them all to us, like all good...mothers," he said awkwardly.

Sarah sank into the warm, gently whirling water, comfortable enough to let Connor's uneasy moment slide over her head. "Kids love fairy tales—the scarier, the better. You say you left the bedroom door open?"

"Mmm-hmm. She'll find us."

Dannie let them have fifteen minutes of peaceful soaking, and then she wandered in, sleepy-eyed, calling, "Mommy?"

"In the bathroom, sweetheart."

She padded to the doorway, blinked, yawned and then blinked again. "Uncle Connor, why are you in the bathtub with Mommy?"

"This isn't a bathtub, Princess. It's kind of a little swimming pool." He motioned to her with a dripping hand. "Come up here and see."

A peek in the tub made her smile. "It's like my Tommy Turtle pool. But you're too big to swim in here."

"It's just for sitting and soaking," Sarah explained. "Take off your nightgown and jump in."

Dannie crossed her arms over her chest, protesting that panties would not be enough. "Go put your swimming suit on, Princess," Connor suggested. "This is just a big family bubble bath."

His choice of words put an end to Dannie's doubts, but for Sarah, the doubts resumed their niggling.

Connor spent much of the morning playing with Dannie, taking great pleasure in producing toys from the closet and pretending not to have known they were there. Sarah and Dannie set up a sandwich bar for lunch while Connor worked out in his private gym. He insisted the key to his fitness program was planned irregularity. With the promise of another horseback ride, Dannie agreed to take her nap, a practice she had begun to think she might have outgrown in just the last week.

"I need some inspiration, Sarah, love."

Sarah found herself being scooped along under Connor's arm toward the music-room door. "Oh, nice. Do I get a private concert?"

"Worse. You get to listen to me struggle through some new music."

Struggle seemed an apt description. It would certainly have been a struggle for her if she had to manage all that equipment. Sarah sat quietly on the couch and listened while Connor took his place at the beautiful baby-grand piano and played through several songs. He used no sheet music, but, of course, some of the songs were his own. Then he turned on a tape recorder and worked with a melody that was obviously in the making. There were many false starts, subtle changes, replays, all recorded on tape. When he'd played the same melody through several times, he turned to her. "What do you think?"

"I think it's lovely."

"Aw, come on." He hooked a hand over his thigh and leaned on his arm. "What does it sound like?"

"It reminds me of a summer night's breeze and a white porch swing, and oars dipping in and out of calm water, silver moonlight slithering bank to bank."

He raised his brow, turning his mouth down slightly as he nodded. "You're right. That's what it sounds like." He saluted her appraisal with a single finger. "There might even be lyrics in what you just said."

"Really? What *I* said?" She beamed. "Write it down before you forget."

"I never forget," he said, touching his temple. "Besides, it's all on tape. Here's the part I don't like." He played several bars from the melody, played them again and shook his head. "It isn't right."

"That's the part with the oars," she said thoughtfully. "Maybe they need to drip a little bit."

He grinned, played with several changes in the notes and finally pronounced, "That's it! They just needed to drip a little bit."

"You work with imagery, too, don't you?"

He shrugged, swinging his knees in her direction. "I guess so. I can't *tell* anybody how it works. I've been asked, and when I can't explain it in words, people get very impatient and start asking easier questions, like, 'How's your love life?' All I can do is *show* somebody how it works, and either they tune in or they don't." He gave her a warm smile. "You, sweet Sarah, are a kindred spirit."

"I'm an artist, Connor. So are you."

He liked that. She was not a popular artist; she'd had little recognition in the art world. But she was serious about her work, she was good at it and she'd put him in her class—the class of serious artists. He reached behind the piano for a twelve-string that stood waiting in its stand. "This is something I've been working on, too. I want you to hear it," he said, chording softly before he sang:

Hey, lady with the paint and the brushes
Pretty lady with the warm brown eyes
What color do you use to make your music?
Oh, lady, can you paint me a song?
Does your soft pink kiss brighten with your
passion?

Will you touch me with cool blue
Like the ocean waters do?
My lady, can you paint me a song?
Give me red from your palette, I'll make fire
Give me gold, give me silver, I'll make love
Paint me what you feel, and I'll make you a deal
I'll sing you a picture while you paint me a song.

He watched his hands play the chorus through again, postponing the quiet for just a moment. But then it came, the silence echoing in his ears. He stared at his hands and heard no applause, no approving words. Finally, he took a deep breath and looked over at the couch. He saw tears.

"That bad?" he ventured gently.

She shook her head vigorously. "That good. That beautiful, Connor. Tell me I really gave you that idea."

"Of course you did." He returned the guitar to its stand and went to her, stooping down in front of her and dropping one knee to the floor. The fingers of his left hand brushed wetness from her face, and she felt the calluses of his finger pads. "Tell me this means I really touched you with my song."

"Of course you did," she whispered.

Leaning forward, he kissed first one eyelid, then the other. "Sweet, sweet Sarah," he chided tenderly. "You're supposed to applaud at the end. You're not supposed to cry."

She laughed through the tears. That's what she'd planned to do at the end—a little applause, a graceful exit, certainly no tears. Obviously it wasn't going to work that way. Wiping her eyes quickly, she pointed to an instrument on the far side of the room. "What's that?" she asked with forced enthusiasm.

"What?" He pivoted on the balls of his feet. "Oh, that. That's a synthesizer. Here, I'll show you how it works."

With one ear Sarah listened to the machine that had a mynah bird's capacity for imitating the sounds of a whole range of instruments—strings, reeds, brass, percussion. Seated in front of the keyboard, Connor demonstrated it for her like a kid putting his model train through its paces.

Her attentive ear made note of his explanation as well as his enthusiasm. Her other ear listened to her heart, which warned her that it was leaving her for this man. Impossible! Don't you realize who he is? Don't you realize what he is? Well, it didn't matter. There was no reasoning with the heart. It knew only the flesh-and-blood man, not the eight-by-ten glossy.

"I'm having a computer system put in," he was telling her. "They've come up with this outfit that stores the music, plays it back for you, even prints everything out on staff paper. Some people like to see everything on paper." The look over his shoulder told her he knew she was one of those. "It'll probably take me a while to get the hang of it, but the saleslady said she'd come out and give me lessons."

Unbidden, an image of the "saleslady" popped into Sarah's mind—a voluptuous computer whiz, California blond and tan. She joined the ranks of the "decorator lady," the housekeeper and the lovely Miss Buffalo in Sarah's mind. She turned up a very un-

Sarahlike, narrow-eyed smile. "How considerate. How many lessons does she suppose you'll need?"

Connor's eyes danced. "She said she'd spend as much time with me as it took. Those manuals are useless, as far as I'm concerned."

"And so impersonal."

Grinning, he stood before her and studied her closely. "I think your eyes are turning green, Sarah. Yes, I do believe they're...and look! Your skin's taking on a greenish cast. Good Lord, woman, what have you been eating?"

He had her. She pursed her lips and then allowed a genuinely sheepish smile. "Witch's brew."

"Eye of newt and toe of frog?" he teased. "Powerful stuff. Know what the antidote is?"

"I'm sure *you* do."

"Of course." He slid his arms around her with a satisfied smile. "It's true love's kiss." His lips were firm, reassuring, slightly moist as he gave her just a single kiss. "True love invites no jealousy, sweet Sarah. And it harbors none."

"Mmm, very quotable. I'll remember that." And the kiss, she thought, savoring the taste of it—I'll remember that, too.

With his finger, he traced a line around her chin, preparing his proposal in his mind. "Let's take Dannie back to her grandparents and let them spoil her for a couple more days while we take a jaunt out to Nashville."

"Nashville?"

"Very short recording session. There are some people I want you to meet there, too, and some great places to—"

"No, Connor. That won't work."

"Why not?"

She pushed her hands against his chest, needing room to think, but he wouldn't give it to her. "First, because Dannie doesn't know her grandparents that well yet, and I'm not sure they're ready for any more of her just now, either."

"And second?"

"Second—" she shook her head, pulling firmly away from him now and moving toward the window across the room "—secondly, I don't fit in. I didn't at the hotel in Springfield, and I won't in Nashville. I won't fit in with that scene anywhere, Connor."

"That was a road party, Sarah. I don't blame you for walking out on that. I don't fit in most of the time at those things, either."

"That's ridiculous. How can the cornerstone not fit in? That's your life, Connor, your career. It's part of you." Fixing her attention on the ocean, she tried to sound matter-of-fact. "This is just an interlude. Pleasant as it's been, we have to be realistic and call it that."

"An interlude?" he repeated slowly, making the word sound like something he didn't want to touch.

She turned to face him, but she put the piano between them. "An interlude with your brother's . . . with your *dead* brother's . . ." There was no putting a name to it. "No matter what the Biblical injunctions are, you have no responsibility for me, Connor. I don't belong in your world."

He followed her around the piano, and when she tried to back away, she backed into the guitar stand. She reached to steady it, and he snatched the opportunity to grab her shoulders and pull her up to face him, nose to nose.

"You and I were alone together last night, Sarah, in *my* house, in *my* bed. You are not my brother's anything. If what you told me this morning was true, you never really were."

She flushed, and her eyes darted away from him. "I bore his child," she reminded him.

"He never knew his child. He never loved her. But I do." Her eyes flashed his way again. "Yes, *I* do, Sarah. Dannie's never had a father. She wants one—needs one. She needs *me*."

"Is it really...Dannie you want?"

His eyes became ice-blue crystal. "You could ask me that?" He loosened his grip on her, and her shoulders sagged. "Yes, I guess you could if you could choose a word like 'interlude.'"

"Connor...you're a man who belongs to a lot of people, and I'm a woman who belongs to very few. It's not just the concerts and the parties and the bright lights. It's...it's Spider Woman and Decorator Lady and all the swooning Gidgets...and Marlene."

He gave her a dark frown. "Who's Marlene?"

"The woman in the picture in your mother's tabloid."

Marlene was dismissed with a gesture of disgust. "I don't even remember that woman."

"You see what I mean?"

"No, I don't see what you mean. Do you know why? Because you don't even see what you mean." He reached for her shoulders, more gently this time. "I'm not the 'interlude' type, Sarah. You do know that. You're having trouble looking me in the eye because you know that."

A sigh told him he was right. "And I'm not the jealous type, Connor, but knowing that beautiful women throw themselves in your path every day...I'm just being realistic."

He pulled her into his arms and touched her hair, letting his fingers trail the length of it. "I think I know what you're afraid of, and it isn't Spider Woman. It certainly isn't Marlene. Just give me a little more time with you. Let me show you there's nothing to be afraid of."

"I'm not afraid, Connor. I'm just extremely practical."

He lifted her face in his hands and gave her half a smile. "You're lying to me, sweet Sarah. I know what it means to be afraid, and you're scared to death. If you won't go to Nashville with me *this time*, will you wait for me? I'll only be gone a couple of days. Three at the most."

"I have work to do at home," she reminded him.

"You can work here. Santa Cruz is a regular haven for artists. We can find anything you need there."

"I have a housekeeping business that won't be around anymore unless I..."

"Oh, forget that," he urged, squeezing the tops of her shoulders. "Your real work is your painting. You're wasting your time and talent pushing a vacuum cleaner around other people's carpets." He knew instantly, by the cold look she gave him, that he'd said the wrong thing. "Listen, Sarah, I admire your ingenuity, but I also admire your talent, and I...will you wait for me?"

"Connor, I can't stay that much—"

"I'll make it two days. I swear." He planted a hard kiss on her mouth, assuming, in typical male fashion, that he'd sealed a bargain. "I need more time with you. I want to show you how it can be." He kissed her again, and she concentrated on how it was.

The night air hung thick and heavy over Sarah, but standing in the dark at the bedroom window, Connor pronounced it remarkably clear and calm. He'd offered her gentle lovemaking, but she'd responded with an urgency that had ignited them both and threatened to set the bed ablaze. She wanted nothing to do with rest or sleep—no part of anything that would steal this time.

"Come to the window, Sarah. I want you to see something."

Sarah slipped into a filmy peignoir before she joined him. Stepping behind her, he gathered her shoulders between his hands and pointed her toward the north, past the twinkling lights of Santa Cruz toward a light blinking in the distance. "You can't always see it from here," he said. "Only on beautifully clear nights."

"A lighthouse?"

"Yes. It marks the point where the ocean meets Monterey Bay. Sometimes I stand here at night and watch it for hours, especially when I feel like taking perverse pleasure in being sorry for myself."

"Sorry about what?"

He draped his arms around her like a shawl, and she hugged them to her. "I get lonely, and that gives me an excuse to feel sorry for myself."

"That light blinking out there in the night..." she observed. "That's the image of loneliness."

"It is when you want it to be. It was built by grieving parents in memory of a son who'd drowned."

"It's an appropriate warning, then."

"Watch it closely, Sarah. What does it warn against?"

The light blinked several times before she answered. "To be careful. Not to get in over your head."

"Ah, Sarah," he chided. "That's just what a lonely person sees, and it's a sure bet that he'll stay lonely if that's the way he chooses to interpret the message. When I interpret it that way, the lighthouse mocks me. It says, 'Wallow in it, then, Ryan. You think you're drowning in your sorrows. Stand up, man! You're only up to your ankles. You don't need me.' And then it goes away."

"It goes away?"

"The next night. Damned if it doesn't shroud itself in clouds the next night." He chuckled at the incredible truth.

"Look!" Sarah pointed to another light blinking offshore. "A boat."

"Coast guard, probably."

"It looks like they're talking to each other."

"I'm sure they are. I'm sure that lighthouse is a welcome sight to any sailor about to put in for the night."

She lowered her cheek and rubbed it against his arm, wishing he could be a sailor or a lighthouse keeper or almost anything but what he was. A performer. A *theatrical person*. "What's the lighthouse's true message, then?" she asked.

"It's a reminder," he told her. "Its beacon spears through the darkness and reaches out to the living. It doesn't say, 'Be careful.' It says, 'Take care.'" He turned her in his arms. "Take care of me, Sarah." Bending to her, he whispered close to her mouth. "Let me take care of you."

He took her to his bed, and she took him deeper inside herself than she had thought possible. She had never been in touch with herself as he was. She had never let herself know the softness she kept locked away in a spiritual package. But Connor knew it. He found it, and he opened it up and kissed it with the hard part of himself—the part of a man that must complete itself with woman's softness. He made Sarah whole in a way she knew that she would never be whole again without him.

The following day he left for Nashville, and Sarah knew that if she waited for him to come back, she'd never be able to leave him.

Chapter Nine

Moving from Connor's world back to her own was predictably depressing. Sarah told herself it was obviously because she'd broken the cardinal rule for maintaining contentment among the common folk. Ordinary people should never fraternize with the rich and famous. She found that she was lecturing herself aloud, trying to banish from her brain all thoughts of bedrooms with hot tubs and views of the ocean. She wasn't a California girl, and she never would be. She needed that good, solid New England...composure. Yes, that was it, and Massachusetts reliability and fierce Yankee independence. Those were sterling traits, tried and true. She was in tune with those things, and she wouldn't have the machinations of the entertainment industry fouling up good metabolism.

But when the phone rang ninety-six hours to the minute after she'd stepped on New England soil again, she had a premonition. It seemed unlikely that the heart could stop and the pulse race simultaneously, but Sarah's did.

"Sarah? Connor. You left Dannie's pants with the dolphins on them."

"Oh." Deep breath. Steady. "Yes, she's been asking for them. Maybe you could..."

"I knew you'd taken off. I called home from Nashville a couple of times. Let the phone ring off the hook."

"I'm sorry. I thought it was best... I tried to explain before you left, but... We did have a wonderful time. I wanted you to know that."

"Oh, yeah? A wonderful time? Sounds like a post-card."

Sarah bit her lip and squeezed her eyes shut. She was botching this. "Anything I say will sound inadequate. That's why I left without saying anything."

"I swore I wasn't going to call, but I decided that was foolish. No team has room for more than one grand-stander, and you've laid claim to that position."

"That's hardly a fair description. I told you I couldn't stay. You wouldn't accept that, and I just... well, I didn't want to argue with you."

She heard him expel an impatient breath, and she imagined a cigarette in his hand. "I guess I misread you," he said. He sounded hard and unemotional. "When you described what we had as an 'interlude,' I thought you meant that as an accusation, not a confession."

Her voice tightened. "What are you saying?"

"I'm saying you made it an interlude by taking off like that. I had every intention of making it much more."

"What more could it be?" she asked quietly.

"Unless you're very good at faking it, you know the answer to that."

Of course. They'd had good sex. "I'm sorry, Connor, but the answer eludes me. Perhaps I have a limited vocabulary in that respect. I'm not sure what the word is for prolonging an interlude. Would you call it an affair?"

"An affair?" he rejoined with disgust.

"Whatever the arrangement might be called, it wouldn't work. I have a four-year-old daughter. For most men, that's excess baggage."

"But we both know I'm not most men."

She sighed. "Yes, we do. You've been good to Dannie every minute you've spent with her, and if you can ... find more time to spend with her, I think ..."

"*Find more time!* That's what I asked you to do, Sarah. I asked you to find more time for me—for us. I'm not interested in an affair. If I wanted an affair, I'd call Maureen, or whatever her name is." He'd let an urgency creep into his voice that he didn't like. He paused for control. "I was thinking we could call the arrangement 'marriage.' Does that term give you any trouble?"

Marriage to Connor Ryan. Oh, God. The man she loved was proposing marriage. She'd expected almost any other possibility, but not this one. It didn't fit with what he was. With *who* he was, yes, but not with what he was.

"Apparently I just told a bad joke," he said quietly. "I'm getting no response."

"It . . . it couldn't work, Connor," Sarah managed, the tears burning in her throat.

"You've said that before. It makes me wonder whether you have a crystal ball up your sleeve." She knew he was dragging on that cigarette again, and she felt the smoke crowding her own chest. "Okay, read the tea leaves for me. Why wouldn't it work?"

"Because you're Connor Ryan."

"And you don't want to be married to Connor Ryan," he presumed, knowing somewhere in his gut that wasn't true.

"I don't want to be married to a life-style that terrifies me," she said.

"I'm not asking you to marry my life-style. I want you to marry *me*. My life-style right now is that of a bachelor. If we were married, that would change. Your life-style would change. We'd come up with a new one that suited both of us."

Sarah pressed her hand back and forth across her forehead, which was beginning to throb with the effort of holding back her tears. The pictures that flashed behind her eyelids were of a man she wanted very much to be with, a man who sang his heart out in a crowded auditorium and in a quiet room—a man who gave one child a seashell and another his autograph. And then, God forbid, there was a man selling detergent on TV, and she was angry and heartbroken both, but the truth was, she'd wanted to be with him, too.

"There's more to your life-style than that, Connor. There are things you cannot change as long as you are what you are."

"Look, Sarah, my private life is my own. I don't belong to my career like...like Kevin belonged to the army. My music isn't a life-style; it's a life force, and it has been since I was a kid. That's part of me, part of who I am and who I was long before Georgia Nights. I know you understand that. You understand it better than anyone I know."

"Yes," she whispered, "I do understand."

"Then why do you have trouble accepting me as I am?"

"I don't. I love you as you are."

"Marry me, then," he entreated quietly.

"I can't, Connor. You're a star. You can't come down to earth for me, and I'm afraid of heights."

"That's crazy talk, Sarah, and I won't accept it. But I won't prolong the argument, either. I'll be in touch."

He hung up the phone thinking he'd be in touch after he'd given her some time to be without him. She belonged with him, and he'd give her a few months to realize that. She'd miss him. Within four weeks, she'd gladly live in Grand Central Station with him if he asked her to. He'd give her an extra month or two just to make sure she felt exactly the way he was feeling right now. Damned miserable.

It worked. No one could have been more miserable in the weeks to come than Sarah was—unless, of course, it was Connor. Sarah's housekeeping business thrived, partly because of the holiday season and partly because she took to cleaning with frustrated furor. Her painting was another story. She wasted a lot of canvas. One fruitless afternoon ended with neat pats of blue and yellow paint splattered on the wall, where she'd dashed her pallet pad, and with one previously neatly stretched canvas lying on the floor, its frame broken over the radiator. New England composure had bitten the dust.

Connor, on the other hand, did some of his best writing when he was miserable. Sadness had always given him a different kind of voice, one that the dyed-in-the-wool country-music fans identified with. Since he was feeling sorry for himself, his lighthouse wouldn't talk to him, so he holed up with his piano and nursed his loneliness. It made for good melancholy music.

While Connor nursed melancholia, Sarah brought her instinctive mother's nursing skills to bear on Dannie, who had come down with a cold when they returned to California. It simply wouldn't go away. Sarah blanketed it and misted it, doused it with vitamin C and baby aspirin, but the cold hung on while the coughing got worse. California seemed to have taken its sunny toll, draining the hardiness and composure right out of both of them.

When Connor called again, it was because he'd seen a Christmas tree with a Raggedy Ann doll sitting underneath it in a department-store window. He'd stood in front of the window for a long time, and then he'd bought a bottle of whiskey. He never drank whiskey, but Raggedy Ann had that effect on him. Whiskey and water was a man's drink, or so he'd heard. He laughed out loud and toasted the image of his father, who stood off in the corner of his mind, nodding approval. Had he given her enough time? Would just the sound of his voice make her shiver inside her flannel painter's shirt? Hell, he wasn't about to grovel. He just wanted to talk.

"Sarah? Connor. How's it goin'?"

"Connor? It's . . . I . . . it's good to hear your voice."

He shivered inside his sweatshirt and fortified himself with another bitter swallow. Keep it casual, he reminded himself. "Is it? Same here. So how's it goin'? You ready for Christmas?"

"Christmas?" His voice sounded as though it was listing a little to one side.

"Yeah. Have you decked the halls yet?"

"No. Not yet. Connor, are you drunk?"

"Gettin' there. I was . . . just out with some friends," he lied. He wanted her to think there was good reason for his condition, and he didn't want her to think she had anything to do with it.

"I see. You start your Christmas parties early out there."

"We've gotta do something. We don't get much snow." Another sip, and he set the glass down. It tasted like sewer water. "I called to ask you . . . what are you wearing?"

"What am I . . . a T-shirt and jeans."

"And a huge flannel shirt with paint all over it?"

She looked down. "Yes."

His laughter was warm and rich. "I thought so, but I had to make sure."

"Why?" she asked, too enraptured by the sound of his voice to worry about him making any sense.

"Because that's what you were wearing the first time I saw you, and I was just thinking how that outfit impressed me. Do you know, I can't remember what Miss Buffalo wore with her crown, but that big flannel shirt was great on you.''

"And how is . . . Marlene?"

He chuckled. "Cold if she's in Buffalo. They're getting snow. It's supposed to miss you, but you may get some flurries tonight." The fog he'd tried to surround himself with wasn't thick enough. He was seeing her face. "Are you . . . cold, Sarah?"

"Yes," she said quietly.

"I am, too." He let the silence give him some breathing space before he picked up a conversational tone. "How's my Princess?"

"She's in bed with . . . she isn't feeling well."

"Not feeling well? What's the matter?"

As if on cue, Dannie called for Sarah from her room. "She's had a cold. Connor, I have to go. She's . . ."

"Put her on the phone. Just let me say hello."

"I really don't . . . I hate to get her up just now," Sarah hedged.

"Sarah, what's wrong?"

There was no trace of drink in his voice now. She'd alarmed him. "Nothing, really. She's calling for me, so I really have to . . ."

"Go on upstairs. I'll hold on."

"But it may be—"

"I said I'll wait." He could just as easily call her back, but somehow he couldn't bring himself to break the connection.

When she returned to the phone, she sounded distressed. "She wanted water. I've told her not to get out of bed. I'm sure it's one of those things that has to run its course, but that cough has me worried."

"Has she seen a doctor?" he wondered.

"I have an appointment for tomorrow morning." The racking cough started again upstairs. "Oh, Connor, she's having another coughing spasm. I have to go."

"I'll call you tomorrow," he promised. He hung up and lit a cigarette. Inexplicably, the lungful of smoke pinched his chest inside. Reaching past his unfinished drink, he snuffed out the cigarette. Late morning tomorrow? Noon tomorrow? When would she know something? Late morning there would be early morning here, but he couldn't wait that long. He made one more phone call and then heaved himself out of the chair and headed for the bedroom.

Chapter Ten

Connor remembered the feeling he'd had the first time he'd pulled up in this driveway. He'd been suspicious, true, but something had told him that what lay behind that door would change his life, and that thought had scared him. He hadn't minded the prospect of sitting on the hot seat in Kevin's behalf. How many times had Kevin done just that for him? What had scared him, even as it attracted him, was the image of that porcelain face and the feeling that what started out in Kevin's behalf might soon be in his own. Kevin had nothing to do with this now. It was Connor's little girl who was sick, and it was Connor's woman who needed his help, even if she was too damned stubborn to admit it.

The house looked like a forbidding sentry, its dark upper-story windows staring emotionlessly at the snow-covered front yard. Connor mounted the porch steps and tipped his head back for a look overhead. Gray-white clouds moved swiftly past the gray shingles of the gable above him. He shouldn't have called her three sheets to the wind. But if he hadn't, he might not have called at all, and then he wouldn't have known. She'd never have called him. Sarah was used to taking care of everything herself. That was something he'd come here to change if he could. She was going to start seeing him differently. The door knocker clattered under his fist.

"Hey, Connor, Sarah didn't say anything about you coming out. Come in, come in." Grinning and bright eyed, Jerry swung the door open wide and gestured for Connor's entry. "He-e-ey, great to see you. Dannie's been talking about California nonstop since they got back, and Sarah sure had a good time. Is Sarah in for a surprise, or was she just keeping me in the dark about you coming?"

Connor stripped off his leather gloves and offered a quick handshake. "She's in for a surprise. How's Dannie?"

Jerry's face settled immediately into an expression of concern. "I really don't know, man. Sarah just called. She says the doctor suspects pneumonia. They're admitting her into the hospital, I guess."

"What hospital?"

"Oh, geez, I forgot to ask. She'll probably be calling back later, though. We'll get the whole story then. Poor kid's been pretty sick." The solemnity on Jerry's face brightened with his next thought. "Say, how about a beer? Sarah said she might not be home for a couple of days, and she wanted me to watch the house, so I stocked up.''

"No, thanks.'' An impatient wave of the hand dismissed the offer. Why hadn't this boy made it his business to find out a little more? "How long has she been pretty sick?''

"Well, she's had this cold, see. You know how kids get in the winter—nonstop runny noses, always coughing and sneezing.'' Jerry shoved his hands in his pockets and edged toward the living room. He figured if Connor didn't want a beer, he wouldn't have one, either. "Anyway, it's been hanging on. Sarah said she was up all night with her last night.''

"Who's her doctor?''

Jerry wrinkled up his face and thought a moment. "Gee, I don't know that I've ever heard her mention a doctor. Dannie's not a sickly kid—nothing ever that serious. Sarah takes real good care—''

"All kids go to the doctor once in a while,'' Connor informed him as he pulled a soft plaid muffler like a bell cord, sliding it off his neck and tossing it on a chair in passing. "Sick or not. Where would Sarah keep a list of important phone numbers?''

"I don't know. Probably—'' Connor was already rifling through the small drawer under the telephone table "—in that drawer,'' Jerry finished, shrugging.

Connor found the list he was looking for inside the front cover of the phone book. A call to the pediatrician's office turned up the name of the hospital.

"You're going to show me how to get there, Jerry. We're driving over together.'' The little drawer swallowed up the phone book as the receiver whacked into place under Connor's hand.

"Sure thing. It's only a few miles." Jerry returned to the front entry and took his nylon parka down from the coat tree. "Did you rent a car?"

"Yeah. Listen, Jerry." Connor took pains to lay a friendly hand on Jerry's shoulder, and Jerry was all ears. "I want you to go with me to the hospital and wait around there for a while until we have some idea what's going on."

"Oh, yeah. Sure thing."

"Sarah's probably exhausted, and I'm going to try to talk her into coming home with you later. I want her to let me stay with Dannie while she gets some rest. Will you do that for me?" Jerry nodded. He liked the idea of doing Connor a personal favor. He could see himself taking on other jobs, acting in some official capacity in behalf of Connor Ryan. He could probably become his personal adviser or bodyguard.

"It may take a while," Connor warned. "She'll think she has to do it all herself. But you'll hang in there with me, won't you?"

Nodding again, Jerry grinned. "'Course, she'll probably say she can drive herself." But nobody could say Jerry hadn't *tried*. Driving his sister around was a far cry from being a bodyguard. Willingness was what the man was looking for, obviously.

"Undoubtedly. But we're going to take care of *her* for a change. We're going to persuade her that she doesn't have to carry the whole world on her own little shoulders."

Jerry agreed. He liked the sound of that. It sounded pretty tough. He'd *insist* on driving Sarah home. Then he'd personally see to it that she got some rest.

Northampton Hospital was not far from Sarah's home in Amherst. Connor bypassed the directory on the wall and went straight to the reception desk for directions. The receptionist ran her finger through a list and shook her head. Dannie had apparently not been admitted yet.

He found Sarah in a waiting area holding her little girl in her arms. Wrapped as she was in a pink-and-blue blanket, Dannie seemed much smaller than Connor remembered. They both looked as though they should have been in bed, but Sarah brightened visibly when she saw him, whispering something to Dannie as he approached.

Sarah had thought of him often since he'd called, thinking he wouldn't be able to get hold of her at home and she'd have to try to call him as soon as she knew something. She hadn't allowed herself the hope of seeing him. He looked like heaven. He wore a camel topcoat, which hung open over a camel blazer and rust slacks. Only once before had she seen him in a dress shirt and tie, and she'd thought that effort had been made for his parents.

Wisps of hair the color of winter wheat dipped over his forehead, and he ran a hand through them quickly before he crouched next to Sarah's knees, offering both his girls his most winning smile. "I took the first flight I could get. I brought Dannie's pants, too."

Dannie offered the best smile she could muster, though her usual exuberance wasn't there. Sarah watched as Connor touched Dannie's wild blond curls, remembering how he'd done that so tentatively the first time he'd seen her. He cupped the child's cheek in his hand and kissed her forehead, his tenderness taking a tight hold in Sarah's own heart. When he lifted his eyes to hers, she couldn't speak. Her chest hurt with the effort of holding back the words, "Thank God you're here."

The words were in her eyes, and Connor read them. "You look tired," he said gently.

Sarah closed her eyes and nodded.

"I'm sick, Uncle Connor. The doctor says they can make me well if I stay here a little while."

Connor shifted his gaze to Dannie and smiled. "They've got all kinds of great stuff here, Princess. They've got medicine and pretty nurses to give it to you so you'll get better."

"Mommy gives me medicine," Dannie insisted. She looked much too pale, and her lips seemed dry and chalky.

"I know, and she's just as pretty as any nurse." He offered Sarah a reassuring wink. "Prettier, even. But she's not a nurse. And here in the hospital, the nice doctors tell the pretty nurses what kind of medicine to give and how much. They've got it all worked out."

"Is that lady over there a nurse?" Connor followed Dannie's finger to a white-uniformed woman behind the desk. Her cap identified her as a nurse, and Connor nodded. "Well, she isn't pretty," Dannie judged.

"No, she isn't," he agreed. "But I'm sure she's nice."

"She isn't nice, either. She won't let me in here."

Connor glanced up at Sarah, frowning slightly. "I don't know what they're doing back there. Probably checking our credit. I told them I had enough money to pay them, but they want insurance," Sarah explained, trying to make it sound like a minor inconvenience. The "minor inconvenience" had left her sitting here with a sick child in her arms for almost an hour.

"You don't have health insurance?"

"No. I know I should have, but I've managed to... I've been putting it off," she confessed.

"Has the doctor sent the order to admit her?"

"Yes. They said it would be just a matter of... getting a little more information or something. They needed some different forms and somebody else's signature."

"I don't want to stay here, Uncle Connor," Dannie whined pathetically. "I want to go home."

Connor patted her little hand before he rose to his feet. "Your mommy and I will stay with you, honey. I'll see if things can't be—"

"Connor," Sarah began, "There's no need for you to..."

He smiled encouragingly. "Where else am I going to stay? I came to visit you, and here you are. Besides, I *love* hospitals. They're so... clean. Who do you suppose does their housekeeping?" He couldn't resist taking Sarah's chin in his hand and bending to kiss her, briefly but firmly. "Let me take care of the nice lady at the desk, and then we'll call for the bellman."

Jerry joined the group, having parked Connor's rental car with special care. He handed Connor the keys just as Connor headed for the admitting desk. Then Jerry gave Sarah and Dannie each a loving pat on the shoulder and settled into a chair with two well-thumbed copies of *Road and Track*.

Connor's charm had a way of speeding things up behind the admitting desk. He'd learned long ago that he could get quicker action by lubricating the human cogs in any wheel with a little honey. He used his name, his identification and, on the very pragmatic head nurse, his assurance of payment of all expenses, a responsibility that he assumed gladly and in writing. It was gratifying and handy to find that people who were screaming fans of his by night were actually very dignified hospital personnel by day.

Sarah and Dannie were suddenly whisked to a private room in the pediatrics wing. One minute they'd been set aside in the waiting room, and the next they were being escorted by three nurses and two orderlies, one pushing Dannie's wheelchair, the other buzzing with one of the nurses about "Connor Ryan" and "Georgia Nights."

"Very effective bit of name dropping," Sarah muttered as she and Connor stood out of the way while the nurses fussed over Dannie, provided her with a hospital gown and a plastic bracelet and took her vital signs.

"It's *my* name," Connor reminded her, matching her mutter with a deeper one of his own. "I'm allowed to drop it."

"What else did you drop? A little under-the-table cash?"

Connor shook his head. "I tried that, but Mrs. Morgan would have no part of it. She took my signature, though."

"For what?"

He shrugged. "For posterity."

"Connor, you're not going to pay any..."

"Let's not argue in front of the k-i-d. She's got enough trouble."

"All right," Sarah agreed with a sigh. "We'll argue later."

One of the nurses approached Sarah with an attitude that said she sympathized with Sarah simply because she was the mother of a sick child, which Sarah found somewhat reassuring. She'd begun to wonder whether this was turning into a fan-club meeting. "Dr. Rochard has ordered more tests and another set of X rays, Miss Benedict. We'll want to get those done and then let Dannie get some rest, which is what she needs most right now."

"I intend to stay..."

"One of us will be here as long as Dannie is here," Connor said. He glanced at Sarah. "Whichever one isn't dead on his feet."

"That's fine," the nurse told them. "You might want to find the cafeteria and have something to eat once we have everything taken care of. This little girl is too tired to keep her eyes open, and you look like you could use a break." Her sympathy was again directed at Sarah, who was unaware that the dark smudges under her eyes were a dead giveaway for exhaustion. She did know that she felt like an overwound watch.

Once Dannie was asleep, Sarah agreed to a break. There were a few customers scattered about the tables in the hospital's cafeteria, mostly people dressed in white, reading the evening paper over a cup of coffee. Connor ordered soup and sandwiches for both of them despite Sarah's protests. When they sat down at a corner table, which offered a measure of privacy, she was still protesting. Connor ignored her, setting the food in front of her. She ate, almost as a reflex, and he watched, satisfied. She looked as though she hadn't had a decent meal in weeks. He'd see that she had one soon, but he knew this was the most he'd get into her now.

"I heard one of the orderlies call her 'the Ryan girl,'" Sarah was saying. "I don't know what you told them, but I can't approve of the way you've just..."

"I think they assume she's my child," Connor explained, adding quickly, "I didn't tell them she was. I just...didn't say she wasn't."

Sarah rolled her eyes ceilingward and sighed. "And she calls you 'Uncle Connor.' They must think she's one of those children with all kinds of 'uncles.'"

Connor's lopsided smile was almost apologetic. "More likely, they think I'm one of those Hollywood creeps who isn't married to any of the mothers of any of his children."

"But they appear to be fans, and they adore you despite your little indiscretions." Sarah stared at him a moment. "They can't...you don't think they'd gossip loudly enough for one of those newspapers to get hold of it, do you?"

He shook his head. "Hospital records are out of bounds."

"But speculation..."

"Relax, Sarah." He reached for her hand. "No one knows I'm here. If the press shows up, I'll see that some heads roll. Hospital staff members are generally pretty discreet when it comes to the media. I'm not here for a concert, so no one's looking for me.''

She fixed her eyes on the black face of the watch that peeked out from under the cuff of his shirt sleeve. ''I read in one of those papers last week that you'd been rude to a waiter but that you were to be forgiven because you were trying to quit smoking. The writer saw you at a party two days later with a cigarette in your hand.''

He squeezed her hand, tickling her palm with his fingertips. ''Are you reading that stuff for the same reason my mother does? If you want to know what I've been doing, just ask me, Sarah. I've been out a few times since you left.'' She glanced from their hands to his eyes, betraying her reaction to that news. ''With friends. Not with women,'' he assured her.

''It's none of my business.''

''Then don't look for information in the tabloids. Don't read them at all. That's rule number one.''

She pulled her hand away from his. ''That would be the problem, wouldn't it, Connor? I'd have rules to go by, but there'd be none for you.''

''I'd go by the same rules you would, Sarah. Haven't you noticed by now that I'm pretty damned straight? Why do you think they print stories about me trying to quit smoking?'' She raised a brow at the question. ''Because I don't give them much to write about. The pictures with Miss Buffalo were hard to avoid. The girl wanted some publicity.'' He lifted one shoulder, admitting, ''I let somebody take our picture. No harm done.''

"Are you really trying to quit smoking?" she asked. She realized she didn't want to think about Miss Buffalo.

"Isn't everybody?" He managed to take her hand and get half a smile out of her before he swore solemnly, "I would never let them hurt Dannie . . . or you. You'll be part of my private life, and I never let them touch that."

The concern in his eyes made her want to let go so badly. "I'm sorry, Connor. I don't know why I'm giving you such a bad time. I should be thanking you for getting us out of that waiting room. I should be thanking you for coming. It's just that . . . you've taken everything out of my hands, and I'm not sure I like that."

He opened her hand and smoothed his palm over hers, then cupped his hand under hers. "I haven't taken anything out of your hands, Sarah. I've just put my hands under yours, just to give you a little support."

The touch of his lips to her fingertips brought the tears she'd been trying so hard to dam up. She heard the scrape of a chair and felt him slide up next to her. Without another thought, she turned to him, burying her face against his neck. He rubbed her back while she wept silently. It didn't matter where they were just then or who else might be there. Connor shielded her from the world, and she was free to cry. She believed for the moment that he wouldn't let anything touch her.

Moments later she lifted her head from his shoulder, and he recognized the cue. He handed her a handkerchief. Wiping and sniffling, she eyed the mascara smudge she'd left on his collar. "Oh, look what I've done now. I'm sorry," she said, squaring her shoulders in search of the composure she'd lost.

"Don't apologize for tears," he said quietly, taking the handkerchief from her hand to dab away the dark, wet smudge she'd left under one eye. "Tears are my stock-in-trade. I've written my share of sad songs. I think people should cry more often."

She closed her eyes, and her sigh was quivery. "I'm just tired."

"I know."

"And I'm tired of being tired. Sometimes I hate Kevin for leaving me with all the responsibility. It's supposed to be..." Sarah opened her eyes, surprised by what she'd heard herself say. "Of course, it is my responsibility, and Kevin can't be blamed. He can never be blamed."

"Of course he can. He had no business making you pregnant, Sarah."

Sarah looked up at him, wondering if she'd heard him right. They were both spouting nonsense. "If he hadn't, I wouldn't have Dannie," she reminded him. "He didn't plan on dying within a few months."

"He didn't plan on becoming a father within a few months, either. You know, I don't think it's blasphemous to admit that you hate somebody for dying on you. I think it's normal. I hated him for checking out on me, too."

His arm was still draped behind her chair, and he was rubbing circles around the top of her shoulder with this thumb. Everything he did felt good to her, and everything he said sounded sensible—even what he was saying now, which had to be utter nonsense. "I don't really hate him," she said. "And I'm grateful to him for giving me Dannie."

"I'm grateful for Dannie, too, but I'm honestly not grateful to Kevin for the role he played."

Sarah frowned, tilting her head slightly to the side as though she needed a different perspective. "You're not jealous of him . . . now. Are you?"

Lifting a shoulder in response, Connor sighed. "I don't know. I spent a lot of years envying Kevin. I figured to unload all that the day I proved to him that I was just as good at what I did as he was at what he did." He smiled a little sheepishly. "That was a tall order because Kevin did everything well. But I was just on the verge." His eyes became distant with the memory, his hand poised in the air as though at the edge of something. "Things were just about to happen for me. I wanted Kevin to be there, to see that I really was good and that none of that other stuff mattered because I could make good music."

"What other stuff?" she asked.

He glanced at her, and then glanced away, shrugging again. "Nothing, really. I was never much of a student or anything like that. Kevin was the whiz kid in school. Anyway, he was killed just before Georgia Nights really made it big."

Sarah laid her hand on his thigh. "Kevin told me his brother was a musical genius. He said you could pick up any instrument and play it without a lesson. He said you didn't even need a book."

Connor leaned back into a sardonic laugh. "Didn't even need a book. That's a good one, Kev."

"I'm serious, Connor. Kevin said . . . once when he was complimenting a sketch I'd done, he said he admired anyone who had artistic talent, and then he said it reminded him of his brother. He would've given anything to be able to play the piano the way you did, he said."

Sobering, Connor raised a brow in her direction. "He said that?" A nod confirmed what he already knew was a likelihood. "He would. He should've been there for one concert. Just one. I could've given it all back to him with just one performance."

"Given what back to him?" she wondered.

"The fruits of his labors." He reached past her and snatched the remaining sandwich half from her plate, and she knew he wouldn't explain further.

"I'm not going to make you finish your soup," he promised, waving the sandwich in front of her nose, "because it's full of salt water now. But you're going to finish this sandwich before I send you home to bed."

She accepted the sandwich but shook her head at the rest. "I'm staying. Dannie's liable to have another night like the last, and she'll be frightened if I'm not here."

"I'll be here. She'll ask for you, and she'll get me. She won't be frightened."

Sarah knew it was true. Connor's presence would give Dannie almost the same sense of security her own would bring. In a short time, he had become almost a . . . Oh, no, you don't, Sarah. That's a dangerous thought. "You can come back in the morning, Connor. After you've had . . ."

"A good night's rest? That's what *you* need. You've been at it long enough. Besides, I . . ." He rolled his eyes with a sudden thought. "Damn, I forgot about Jerry. I asked him to wait around and drive you home. I think I've just put his loyalty to the test."

"I can drive myself," Sarah protested. "That is, I *could* if I were..."

Connor smiled. She was weakening. He pushed his chair back and handed her purse to her. "But you don't have to, sweetheart. Your loving brother is standing by. And good ol' Uncle Connor claims the first shift at Dannie's bedside."

"You *are* trying to take over here, Connor, and I won't let you get away with it."

With a firm hand at her waist, he guided her toward the exit. "You're a bit short-tempered right now, Sarah, really not fit company for anyone. But that's only because you're tired. You'll be a brand-new woman tomorrow, one the rest of us won't mind being around."

Sputtering, she allowed herself to be conducted to the waiting room, where Jerry was, sure enough, still waiting to take her home.

Connor sat in near darkness drinking coffee from a Styrofoam cup. The night-light by the bed cast Dannie's face, turned toward him as she slept, in soft relief. Her small features were more pronounced by contrast with the shadows. She looked like Kevin, and Kevin, of course, looked like Connor.

Kevin had been the younger of the two brothers by a year and a half, so it was fair to claim that it was Kevin who looked like Connor. Connor used to wonder why God had made them so alike on the outside and so different under the skin. He remembered thinking once that God had made a mistake with Connor, so He'd made Kevin to see if He could do better the second time.

They'd even sounded so much alike that they were able to fool their mother over the phone. Of course, Kevin couldn't carry a tune in a tin bucket. Connor smiled at the memory of Kevin shouting songs in the shower. It was awful. Their father had laughed whenever he heard it and said that Kevin had a voice "just like his old man—one you could scare a bear with." He never said much about Connor's voice, but his mother had always volunteered him for the boys' choir at every post's chapel.

Connor had started school two years ahead of Kevin, but by the time Connor was eight years old, Kevin was in his class. Kevin had skipped the first grade, and Connor had repeated it. To say that Connor hadn't been much of a student was being generous. His teachers couldn't imagine what the problem was. Connor had a good vocabulary, and he remembered everything that was discussed in class, whipped through his math facts faster than anyone else. But he couldn't read. One teacher finally announced to his mother that Connor simply refused to read, that it was just pure laziness.

Connor wasn't lazy. He wanted to read, but he got mixed up. He hated the way his face would get hot and his throat would burn. There were sounds that were supposed to go with letters, but he couldn't put them together right, and he didn't know why. Then one day at recess he overheard the reason.

In class that morning he'd stumbled through a reading lesson, obediently taking his turn reading aloud, even though it always made his stomach hurt. It had gone pretty much the way it always did. The teacher never made him read very much of the story. He was glad of that because he always understood what the other kids read, but when he took his turn, he never could make any sense out of it. By the time he would struggle to the end of a sentence, the teacher prompting him all the way, he'd lost the meaning. Still, he tried because he didn't want anyone to tell his mother he was lazy again. Dad had spanked him for that.

He kept trying until that one day at recess, when he heard one of the boys in his reading group tell Kevin that his brother was stupid. Connor could still hear the words. "I may be a slow reader, but at least I ain't *stupid* like that big dummy brother of yours."

Connor had never seen Kevin fight with anybody before, but he did that day. Kevin lowered his head like a big-horned sheep and rammed the other boy right in the gut. It was Connor who broke them up. Connor was a head taller than any of the rest of them, and nobody messed with him. He remembered the look in Kevin's eyes when he hauled Kevin off the other boy's chest. It was a look of pity.

Being stupid was different from being lazy. You didn't get whipped for being stupid. You didn't get called on in class, and you never had to read out loud. The bigger Connor got, the less anxious the teachers were to hold him back a grade. After a while, he wasn't even expected to listen in class as long as he didn't disturb anyone. He'd sit in the back of the room, where the tall kids always sat, and he'd examine his latest collection of things he'd found—rocks, leaves, shells, beach glass, even bugs. He never bothered anyone, and no one bothered him. Everyone accepted him as he was—everyone except Kevin.

"You're not dumb, Connor. You're smarter about a lot of things than anybody, even Dad." Even Dad? That was quite a compliment, coming from Kevin. "I don't want you getting any more bad grades." Connor had laughed. "I mean it. I don't want people saying you aren't smart. I'm gonna read all the lessons to you, and you're gonna listen."

Their mother had stopped reading to them after Kevin had learned to read, and by the fourth grade, the teachers weren't reading to them much anymore. At first Connor would have nothing to do with Kevin's plan because Connor was no baby to be read to anymore. But there were things he wanted to know. He wanted to know about rocks, and that led to fossils, and that led to dinosaurs. He wanted to know about shells, and that led to marine life, which led to tides, which led to the moon, which meant the sky was the limit.

Tirelessly, Kevin read to Connor, and Connor watched as Kevin followed the words on the page with his finger. And then something curious happened. Connor began to whisper the words as Kevin read them. One day Connor took over and read a whole paragraph for himself, straight through, and it made sense. Kevin just sat there grinning at him. He'd known all along his big brother was no dummy.

Connor hadn't been quite so convinced as Kevin was, but the world began to look a little different to him. His grades improved. He experimented and found that there were some things he did very well when he put his mind to it. He remembered everything he heard and found that he had a real knack for memorizing whole passages. He was good in math, and whenever there were science experiments or social-studies projects to do, he excelled. He never became a good reader, as Kevin was, but he could get by. Connor preferred to learn about things by handling them. When he was introduced to the piano, it was love at first touch. At that moment, he became a musician.

Kevin's kid. That was why he'd come at first—because Dannie was Kevin's kid. He'd thought he owed it to Kevin. He'd thought that way so many times in the past. But here in the darkness, with only the sound of Dannie's breathing filling his ears, he used Kevin's memory to help him recall the lesson he had the most trouble remembering—Connor owed it to himself.

Connor took a room in a nearby hotel, and when Sarah came to the hospital the following morning, he had breakfast and went to bed. Dr. Rochard examined Dannie that morning and explained that the infection had settled deep in Dannie's lungs, which was giving them something of a problem in determining which pneumonia-causing organism was at fault. During the next three days, Sarah took days, and Connor took nights, but they shared late afternoons and had supper together.

"It's good to have someone to share the burden with," Sarah confessed over hospital-cafeteria coffee.

"It's good to be granted my share without feeling like I have to try out for the debating team."

"It isn't as though I couldn't handle it," she hastened to add. "But it's nice to have someone else feel the same way I do—worry about her the same way. *Almost* the same way."

Connor accepted the amendment graciously. "Almost. I think procreation's designer gave mothers a special province, especially when a child is hungry or tired or sick."

"But when a child is afraid, it's nice to have someone stronger there." Sarah studied her coffee cup. "Dannie said she had a nightmare last night, and she was glad you were around. You make the goblins disappear. It seems I can only chase them back."

"I just held her until she went back to sleep. Sang to her a little."

"Yes, she told me. You sing better than I do, you know."

"I've never heard you sing." He smiled at the thought.

"You don't want to."

"Yes, I do. I want to hear you sing in the shower and whistle while you work." She glanced up, and he caught her eyes with his. "I want to hear you hum while you rock Dannie to sleep. Dannie . . . or another baby." She caught her lower lip between her teeth, but she couldn't look away. "That same designer of procreation made raising kids a two-person job. It's a lot harder when you try to manage it with one."

"I know." But better with just one for sure than with a second who's never there, she thought. He's here now, a small voice said. But he'll be gone tomorrow or the next day, or the day after for sure, and it gets harder each time to let him go.

"I'm not pushing," he told her. "Not now, anyway. I just want you to know what's on my mind."

Dannie's recovery picked up speed once the troublesome bacteria was identified and the antibiotics began to do their work. Connor took her for rides in a wheelchair, taught her the rudiments of checkers and watched more TV than he'd ever hoped to have the time for. They were both becoming restless.

"I can't go to sleep, Uncle Connor. I'm not tired."

"Miss Mackie said, 'lights out,'" he reminded her, pushing the button on her bed to lay her down.

"Miss Mackie, Miss Mackie." She jackknifed to a sitting position, hands out in front of her. "Let's do 'Miss Mary Mack, Mack, Mack.'"

Connor chuckled, pushing her shoulders back to the bed. "I don't know that one."

"Can I draw one more picture?"

"Tomorrow."

"Then you have to read me a story. Mommy always reads me a story before bed. You never do."

Connor swallowed hard and felt a funny twinge in his stomach. "How about if I sing you a story song?"

Dannie popped up again, grinning. "Yes, a song!"

Thank God. His stomach muscles relaxed as he pulled his chair closer to the bed. He started with "There Was an Old Lady Who Swallowed a Fly." By the end of that one, she was giggling so hard he knew he'd have to come up with another to settle her down. He pulled a quiet ballad from his repertoire and noticed that Miss Mackie peeked in three times, lingering on the second and smiling by the third.

An orderly appeared at the door with a boy in a wheelchair, and Connor motioned them in. With the third ballad, he had an audience of seven and a very wide-awake Dannie. He figured if Miss Mackie didn't care, he sure as hell didn't. Poor kid had been sleeping for days. Mrs. Morgan showed up, and Connor thought the party was over until she asked, more timidly than he'd have thought she had in her, for "Misty River Morning." Miss Mackie finally had to call a halt to the show, not because of Connor's singing but because the applause was getting out of hand.

"But it was wonderful," she told Connor after she'd cleared the room. She stayed to help straighten Dannie's bedding and put her books and toys on the shelf. "My, you're a good little artist for a four-year-old," the nurse said, admiring a drawing she'd picked up along with a couple of books.

"Four-and-a-half almost five," Dannie recited. "See? It's the same toy store as that book is about. See all the toys in the windows?"

Gray-haired Nurse Mackie held up the drawing and the book, comparing the two. The child had a good hand. "Yes, I see. But you put the door here, and the boat here, and the..." The woman smiled, handing the drawing to Connor. "It's almost a mirror image. Isn't that clever? Good night, Mr. Ryan. Sleep well, Dannie."

Connor felt the crispness of the paper between his fingers, but he was transfixed for a moment by the empty doorway. *Mirror image.* He lowered his eyes slowly to the page in his hand.

"I made that for you, Uncle Connor. Do you like it?"

The figures blurred in front of his eyes. "I like it very much, Princess. You draw beautifully."

Chapter Eleven

The threat of snow hung heavy just above the roof-tops the day Connor and Sarah brought Dannie home. She fussed when Sarah draped her with an extra blanket, complaining she couldn't breathe, but Sarah flipped the corners of the double wrappings over Dannie's face and muffled further protests. Connor wasn't sure he had the correct end of the bundle upright until it started squirming.

"I don't know what you've got in this package, Sarah, but I hope it isn't supper," he teased, letting Sarah get the door. "It fights back."

"It'll be subdued soon enough." She closed the door behind her and added for Dannie's benefit, "It's going straight to bed."

"No, I'm not!" Connor flipped the blankets back to give Dannie's best mad face a breather. "I'm not going to bed anymore. I'm staying up."

"The doctor thought you could use one more day in the hospital, young lady. I promised you'd go directly to bed without even letting your feet touch the floor."

"And your dainty feet shall not touch the floor, my lady," Connor promised. Having a seat at the foot of the stairs, he proceeded to unwrap his charge, glancing Sarah's way in search of approval as he worked. "But maybe we could compromise on the location of the bed."

"I think I detect a conspiracy afoot." Sarah hung up her coat and turned, straightening her blouse under the waistband of her skirt and wrinkling her nose in a rabbitlike sniff. "And I think I smell something strangely... piney."

Connor winked at Dannie as Sarah edged past them into the living room.

"What... in the world... is all this?"

"Your mother must not get out much," Connor said, raising his voice toward the living room as he hoisted Dannie, caught up the blankets, and followed. "She doesn't even recognize a tree when she sees one. Wasn't she with us when we drove down to Santa Cruz?" Dannie nodded anxiously. "And didn't she see those big green things sticking up from the ground all over the place?"

"A Christmas tree?" Dannie squealed as she was carried through the living-room doorway. "Oh, boy!"

"I want you to be absolutely calm about this, Princess," Connor warned. "Anything that looks like overexcitement is going to get you a ticket upstairs."

"Are we going to decorate it? Can I help? Can I put the angel on top?"

"I take it you have decorations," he guessed, looking to Sarah for approval.

She was holding back all but the gleam in her eyes. "We do have decorations."

"Handmade stuff?" he guessed again. "All very artistic?"

"Mostly. It's still early, Connor. I planned to get a tree next week. You're not dealing with Mrs. Scrooge here."

"I'm one of those kids who can't wait," he explained, his boyish smile giving proof to his claim. "And you've been preoccupied, so I just thought I'd get things going. I have a good eye for trees."

She turned to admire the tree, already standing in a pot and waiting for the festive touches. "It's beautiful," she admitted, "but what's all the rest of this stuff?"

There was a huge wreath, a coil of fresh garland, pinecones, candles, boxes of lights and Sarah wasn't sure what else. "It's just some stuff I ordered for decking the halls," he said.

"Ordered?" Sarah echoed. Connor had obviously been there before he came to pick them up at the hospital. The couch was arranged for Dannie's comfort with pillows and a coverlet. Dannie seemed content to let Connor situate her there, carefully covering her to her chin with blankets.

"I told them it all had to be pretty traditional and that we'd put it up ourselves." He tucked the blankets beneath the cushions, adding, "I didn't think you'd go for an aluminum light show. They did my place in green-and-white paper sculptures last year. Very clean lines, I was told."

"Who's *they*?" Sarah wondered, opening a box of candles and inhaling the bayberry scent.

"The decorator ladies."

"More than one this time?"

"They multiply at Christmastime. But this isn't department-store style, Sarah. This is authentic, old-fashioned New England greenery." He pivoted in her direction, rising to his feet. "I was going to get a tree myself—go out and chop it down with an ax—but they kicked me off the golf course."

Sarah laughed, pulling the box to her chest. "I love bayberry." Her eyes sought his across the room, telling him she loved what he'd done and loved him for *all* he'd done. The sweater he wore was the same shade of blue as his eyes, which shone as brightly as her own. He stood near the fireplace, hands in his pockets, the gift giver awaiting her approval. She wanted to go to him and show him how he'd filled her heart, but instead she clutched the box of candles and offered tentatively, "Will you . . . stay for Christmas?"

He shook his head. "I can't. I have to be in Austin. We're doing a benefit concert that they're televising live on the twenty-seventh."

"Oh, yes. I think you told me that before." She looked down at the box in her hands. This was the way it would be with Connor—the uncle who visited between engagements. It couldn't be any other way. "We'll be able to see you on TV, then."

"Or in person . . . if you want to."

Laying the box back with the others, she took a step back from the evergreen array and from Connor. "No. We'll have our holiday at home. Perhaps another year you'll be able to join us."

He raised a helpless brow. "Christmas is pretty . . ."

"Why can't we have Christmas now?"

Dannie looked pleased with herself. She'd gotten their attention with a good idea.

"Because it isn't Christmas yet," Sarah pointed out. "And in two weeks, when it is Christmas, you'll want to have it again."

"Well, in two weeks Santa Claus will come because he can't leave the North Pole any sooner than that," Dannie acknowledged. She knew by now how this all worked. "But I think we could have some of it now, before Uncle Connor has to go. We could have Christmas dinner."

"We can certainly have decorations now," Connor suggested. "And if somebody opens the boxes behind the couch, I think we can have a little music." Dannie scooted up to take a peek. "Down, girl," Connor warned. "You're not to raise your head off those pillows." He brought several huge boxes to the middle of the floor, all wrapped in red-and-green paper, and then he retreated to get a fire going in the fireplace.

Sarah opened the boxes carefully, certain that each component part of the stereo system was eggshell fragile. With the fire blazing, Connor joined her in the middle of the floor, ripping into the boxes and setting the parts aside for assembly.

"Someone'll be out in a couple of days to wire this in for you and do a little cabinetwork. We'll have to decide where we want the speakers." He was putting things together in the corner of the room, attaching wires and plugging in cords. "Open that other green box, Sarah. We'll put some music on and see how it sounds."

The green box contained an assortment of records and tapes by a variety of artists, including Georgia Nights. "Doesn't your group have a Christmas album?" Sarah wondered as she read title after title on the album covers.

"I'm told we're going to do one next summer, which doesn't excite me too much, but they say it's a real 'down-home' thing to do. They're thinking of calling it 'Silent Georgia Nights.' Can you believe it?" She groaned, and he sent her a grin in agreement. "I think there's a Streisand Christmas album in there."

"What's in that big box?" Dannie wanted to know.

"Put it this way—when you watch the Christmas special, it won't be flickering in black-and-white. Some people are quite taken by the color of my eyes."

"Some people would be quite taken by the color of all the money you flash around," Sarah said. She knew there was no stopping him, but as she handed him a record album she added, "Personally, I think you've gone too far."

Taking the hand that held out the record, he murmured, "I've gone all the way, love. So have you." She looked up at him, and he smiled at the pink tint that rose quickly in her cheeks. "You know how I mean that. There's no hope for either one of us." He slid the record from her hand and touched her lips briefly with an unexpected kiss. Sarah watched him move away from her and told herself it was only the blaze in the fireplace that made the room suddenly feel too warm.

Music soon filled in for conversation while Connor followed Sarah's and Dannie's directions in stringing lights and mountain-scented garland. Sarah brought out a collection of candleholders and bits of wire and cloth, and soon the dining room and the foyer as well as the living room were festooned with gaily trimmed greenery. They made a party of it, snacking on sandwiches, popcorn and eggnog. With candles and colored lights aglow, Connor lifted Dannie to top the tree with a hand-crocheted white angel, and the effect was complete. There was a three-way toast to early Christmases.

Later Sarah and Connor put a sleeping child in her bed and returned to the warm glow of a waning fire and red wine. Connor made a pile of Sarah's sofa pillows on the floor in front of the fireplace, sat down and gave Sarah a distinctly come-hither look, patting the spot on the floor beside him.

Sarah stood her ground. "Ahh . . . I think the atmosphere in here is a bit overwhelming, Mr. Ryan, and if I were a mind reader, I'd say you were thinking I'd be an easy mark about now."

Connor chuckled. "Easy is one thing you've never been, lady. The only thing on my mind right now is talk."

The single brow she raised in response put him in mind of a tempting little vamp, and he wanted to growl and spring. "Okay, so maybe there are two or three other things on my mind, but talk first." Reaching toward her, he entreated her with an outstretched palm, and she came to him, taking his hand and settling beside him in front of the fire.

"Just a friendly talk?" she asked.

"A serious talk. I think it's time you got to know me better, sweet Sarah."

"But I think I know you quite well. As you so aptly put it, we've..."

He dismissed that with a wave of the hand. "You know me well, Sarah, but I want you to know me better than anyone else, living or dead, has ever known me. And then..." *And then, I want you to love me anyway.* "And then, we'll see." He reached back and pulled a folded piece of paper out of his pants pocket. "Here's what I want to talk about."

Sarah set her glass down while Connor sipped at his, watching her as she unfolded the paper and studied it for a moment. "Is this Dannie's work?"

Connor nodded. "She drew that for me from a picture in one of her books. Does it look strange to you in any way?"

Frowning slightly, she puzzled over the drawing. "It looks like Dannie. She always crowds lots of little things into her pictures, fills all the space with funny little figures. It's in pencil, though. She usually uses crayons. Uses color quite accurately, in fact." With a shrug, she concluded, "I've always thought she was sort of a precocious young artist, but then I have a mother's bias."

A mother's bias, he thought. A lovely sentiment and a terrible standard for a child to live up to. How should the question be phrased in order to sneak it past a mother's bias? No preliminaries, he decided, just ask straight out. "Does she often draw mirror images of her subject or put things upside down, inside out, maybe backward?"

The frown returned to her face as Sarah looked at the paper again, and when she spoke, it was with furrowed-brow impatience. "She's not quite five years old, Connor. If you were hoping to hang something of hers in your living room, I'd say you may have to give her a few years."

"You haven't answered my question. Does this look typical of the way Dannie expresses things when she draws?"

"Well, yes, she does have things a little topsy-turvy sometimes, but... What's this all about, Connor? I don't understand what you're getting at. Do you see a problem with Dannie's picture—some Freudian meaning hidden here somewhere?"

"I don't know about Freudian, but I think there might be a problem." Connor draped his forearm over an upraised knee and admired the color of the wine he swirled in his glass. It was something he never discussed with anyone, not since Kevin, and he wondered if he could find a matter-of-fact approach, like Dannie's doctor Dr. Rochard: Your child has pneumonia, but I can take care of it. God, how he wished he could make promises like that. "Have you ever heard of dyslexia?" he asked finally.

"I think so. Isn't it some kind of... brain disorder?"

"They call it a brain *dysfunction*," he corrected, though he knew it was called by even less flattering terms. "It's a learning disability. A person who has it often appears to see some things in reverse."

"You're not saying...you think Dannie's retarded or something?" All of Sarah's maternal instincts armed themselves and came to attention. "Connor, you see how bright she is. How can you think that?"

"I said nothing about retardation. I said learning disabled, and I said I thought it *could* be a problem."

"You're jumping to that conclusion based on one little drawing?" Sarah extended the paper near his face. "Based on *this*? Who are you to say my child's—"

"I'm Dannie's uncle, Sarah. And I'm dyslexic."

The hand holding the paper lowered by slow degrees. "But you're not..."

"No, I'm not." He gave her a knowing smile. "In fact, I'm pretty damned smart."

"I wasn't thinking...I mean I wasn't going to say..." What was she going to say? *Brain damaged.* "I don't need any more brain damage," he'd once told her.

"You *were* thinking 'dumb,' but you weren't going to say it because it isn't a polite word." A gentle laugh said he understood. "The day I knew for sure that I wasn't really stupid, I wanted to send out an announcement. 'We are pleased to announce that Connor Ryan isn't such a big dummy after all.' In fact, I had a mental mailing list."

"Connor, you're...you're a bloody genius, for heaven's sake!"

Again she made him laugh, and it occurred to him this wasn't as bad as he'd thought it would be. He wasn't a kid anymore. He knew who he was and what he could do. "I've been called a 'musical prodigy' and a 'gifted musician,' but never a 'bloody genius.' It has a theatrical ring to it." Another sip of wine fueled his need to tell her everything. "However, I am not a gifted reader. I'm not even a decent reader. I'm sort of a...crippled reader. As a young kid, I was a *non*-reader, and that, let me tell you, makes for a very disabled student."

"What causes it?" Sarah asked, her concern for Connor settling in beside her concern for her daughter.

"I don't think they really know yet. They call it a dysfunction because apparently some of the connections in the brain—the synapses—don't function quite right, sort of like faulty wiring. In my case, some of the messages sent from the eye to the brain get reversed somehow, and the brain registers a reversed image. I don't see the same thing on a printed page that you see."

"But you say you can read."

"I can now, though not with the same fluency you have. What happened was that I learned to compensate. I can't really explain how I do it, but I can tell you that it was mostly Kevin's doing. Kevin helped me learn to read."

Sarah looked at the penciled figures on the paper again, and she felt an awful burning in her throat and around her eyes. She wasn't sure what all this meant, but she didn't like the suggestion that Dannie's brain was any less than perfect. "Kevin had no problem himself, did he?"

"Kevin's only problem was that he had to stick up for his brother all the time." Sarah looked up at him, and the glistening in her eyes made his chest tighten inside. "Kevin had no problem, Sarah, and Dannie may not, either. It's more common among boys than girls, and, as far as I know, there's no real evidence that it's hereditary."

"What should we do?"

He chose to include himself in that "we" and hoped she had meant for him to. "We should have her tested by the best educational psychologist we can find. If she needs help, we'll get it for her. When I was a kid, they didn't know much about this, but things have changed a lot since then. The law is on our side now. All school systems have to provide for learning-disabled kids."

"Your parents, did they...how did they deal with it?"

Connor turned to the fire, letting his mind slide back in time. "I guess they never did," he concluded. "I only know what I do about it after the fact. Moving around with the army from school to school didn't help matters. Kevin always took it in stride, while I fell farther behind. We ended up in the same grade even though I was more than a year older. I hated bringing home report cards. My mother always got this pathetic look on her face, like I'd really let her down, and my dad got disgusted. I don't know how many times I heard, 'Why can't you be more like Kevin?' I figured I was too stupid to be like Kevin and wished everybody would just accept that and leave me alone. After a while they all did, all except Kevin."

Hoping for a glimpse of what he saw, Sarah leaned toward the fire, too. "When did you discover music?"

"When I was about twelve. I was getting along better in reading by then, and I'd gained a little confidence. Music teachers always liked me because I could sing, and I had one music teacher..." He smiled at the memory. "Long dark hair, soft brown eyes. I had the most painful crush on that woman. She found me at the piano in the school music room one day. I was picking out the melody of a song she'd taught us in class. When I told her I'd never had a piano lesson, I thought she'd have a stroke right before my eyes." He glanced sideways at Sarah and chuckled. "Then she sat right next to me on the piano bench, and I thought *I'd* have a stroke. I did everything she showed me. I think I'd have played Chopin on the first try, just to keep Miss Raymond on that piano bench."

"So you've had a lot of practice plying the ladies with your music." Sarah imagined the beautiful boy he must have been, responding to a teacher who finally offered something besides pity or criticism. Miss Raymond must have felt like the miracle worker.

"I didn't have much luck with Miss Raymond. She got married in June that year and broke my heart. But she did persuade my mother that I should have piano lessons. Dad thought it was a waste of time, but Mom stood her ground that time. I picked up the guitar, too. It was such a relief to find something I was good at, and I gave it everything I had. In junior high I picked up drums, trumpet, sax. I made so much noise Dad was ready to throw me out of the house. I ran track and cross-country to keep him off my back."

"In high school, Kevin and I went separate ways. He wore his letter man's jacket, and I wore faded denim.

He took up body building, and I took up smoking. I played in a rock band, and he danced to the music. Dad displayed all of Kevin's trophies in prominent places and stopped talking to me altogether."

"When did you start writing music?" Sarah wondered.

"When I was in high school." He drained his glass and turned to her again, relieved to find that the glistening in her eyes was gone. He searched for pity for himself in those eyes and felt good when he found none. She needed to understand, for herself and for Dannie and maybe even for him.

"I don't *write* music. I compose and record, but I'm inhibited by pencil and paper. My handwriting looks like bird tracks, and I don't even like to think about having to spell words."

She smiled. "You can spell k-i-d pretty well."

"I know the letters, but they never look right on paper. I've found other ways that work for me. From what I understand, there are as many manifestations of dyslexia as there are dyslexics. If Dannie has a problem, she'll find ways that work for her, too."

Stretching out on his side, Connor propped his arm over a plump pillow. "I didn't mean to scare you with this, Sarah," he said. "I would never have told you about myself unless I thought you needed to know."

"Did you think I would think less of you?"

His eyes met hers. "No. Not you."

"If there's a problem . . . with Dannie . . . I want you to help me."

It was the first time she'd asked him for anything. "I will."

"Not for Kevin's sake," she added. "I'm not asking you to take over for Kevin."

His spine grew rigid. "She's more mine than she is Kevin's. Don't you see that yet, Sarah?"

Sarah wanted to agree. She thought of Connor and Dannie exploring the beach for rocks and shells, of them making breakfast together and of Connor putting her to bed. Sometimes Dannie seemed to be more Connor's even than Sarah's. But that was impossible. In practice, he could never become...

"Kevin would have loved her, too," Sarah said.

"Kevin isn't here, Sarah. I am. We both have to stop feeling guilty about that fact." He sighed and consciously relaxed his back, muscle by muscle. "We have to stop stiffening up with guilt every time his name is mentioned."

She was sitting on one hip, her legs tucked to one side, her skirt pulled properly over her knees. He needed to claim her, declare his place with her. He spread his hand over the sleek, rounded part of her calf, rubbing his fingers over the silkiness of her stocking. "You're more mine than you ever were Kevin's," he said quietly. "Does that make you feel guilty, too?"

"It makes me feel foolish," she whispered, shivering under his touch. "I could no more marry you than I could marry the Prince of Wales."

"Don't be ridiculous, Sarah. He's already married."

"And all the king's horses and all the king's men can't keep the press out of his wife's closet."

"They were both born for that," he reminded her. His hand strayed under her skirt and found a silky thigh.

"I wasn't."

"Neither was I. There's nobody in my closet. My house has been empty since you left it." She closed her eyes and enjoyed the warm surge inside her stomach as his fingers crept along their chosen path. "Come back to me, Sarah. I'm not a prince. I'm not a pauper. I'm not even a 'bloody genius.' I'm just a man, and that's the best and the worst of it."

Just a man. Dear Lord, he could turn her inside out, and *that* was the best and the worst of it.

"I need a place to sleep," he told her. Her skirt had become his sleeve as he slid his hand around her hip. "I turned in my key at the hotel. I need a place—" he laid his head in her lap and snaked his free arm around her waist "—to lay my head. Oh, God, if you don't put your hands on me soon..."

On a sharp breath she curled her body around his head and buried her face in his hair. Groaning, he burrowed his head against her belly, hugging her hips with both arms. It was the desperate embrace of lovers whose only certainty was the present.

He released her only to roll on his back and reach for her again. Stretching herself along his side like a cat, Sarah braced herself up on her arms, one planted on either side of his face. Her hair hung over the right side of her neck like dark sheeting, giving them a curtain of privacy as she lowered her mouth to taste the pleasures of his. He responded to her as a man driven by hunger, working his tongue past her lips for a better taste of her. She was warm red wine, and he would drink his fill, enjoying one sweet sip at a time.

Taking her hips in his hands, he moved her over him, pressed his fingers into the roundness of her buttocks and rocked against her until she pulled away from his kiss and arched her neck, gasping his name. The sound of his name in her throat was intoxicating, and he drifted higher on the tension she created in him. He feathered kisses along the pale curve of her neck as he pulsed against her with the slow, steady rhythm of his heartbeat.

"This is . . . really hard," he whispered.

"Yes." Her voice echoed the soft hiss of the antique radiator. "I'll . . . soften it for you."

"Mmm." His smile traced her jawline. "I meant the floor, but I'm not complaining."

"You just said you needed a place to sleep. I suppose you'll be wanting a bed," she teased, dipping her chin for a nip at his ear. She wanted to tease him and increase her power over him, and then she wanted to use her power to give him infinite pleasure, pleasure that he would remember.

"I'll be wanting a variety of things, and they all start with Sarah." Whispered against her ear, her name sounded distant and exotic.

"The guest room is closest," she told him.

"What's wrong with your room?"

She pushed herself up and locked her elbows, giving her tighter contact with his hips. Connor rolled his eyes at the increased pressure while Sarah smiled down on him. "My room doesn't have a view."

"Give me thirty seconds, honey; it'll have a hell of a view."

"Besides, I went to a great deal of trouble to prepare the guest room for you."

"Oh? Did you put in mirrors?"

"No, but I changed the sheets."

Actually, she had prepared for him. A vase of sweet-scented carnations stood on the dresser and a large, unframed canvas hung above the bed. The painting was a lovely montage of small things, the shells and rocks, fossils and seaweed, driftwood and beach glass that fascinated Connor, all done in soft seaside colors. Connor was transfixed by it.

"It's for you, of course."

He turned to her, his eyes brimming with his love for her. She knew him better than anyone, living or dead, and she was there for him.

"I have this to give you, too," she said, stepping into his arms. She held her breath on the end of that confession. There was no helping it. Whatever the word was for this, she knew that whenever he could come to her and touch her as he did now, she would welcome him.

"Your beautiful body belongs to you, Sarah, always. But share it with me." He took her face in his hands and began covering it with gentle kisses, murmuring, "Give me the pleasure of sharing your body."

"I want to drive you wild with pleasure."

He smiled, letting one hand slip along her breastbone, thumbing her buttons open. "How wild?"

"How wild can you be?"

"That depends," he said, pushing the blouse off her shoulders, "on how long you can postpone getting me there."

She tossed her hair back, laughing wickedly as she began bunching his sweater along his ribs. "A challenge," she said. "I love a challenge."

Once she had his sweater off, she worked on his buttons. Undressing each other became a game, but as they neared the finish, the play grew serious. His chest, with its sprinkling of curling gold hair, was still California-sun burnished, while hers, offset by her ice-blue slip, was New England snow. He let her explore the contours of his torso until she discovered she could make his nipples tighten with the light prodding of her fingertips, and he growled and fell back to the bed, taking her with him.

"The light," she said.

"Leave it. Let me see you."

"I'll turn it down," she decided, reaching for the key on the hurricane lamp by the bed. The small light in the base was a suitable compromise.

Connor tucked her under him and began making casual forays along her shoulders and chest with his mouth. He slipped her straps down and released the hook that freed her breasts. It was his wanton tongue that quickened the pace, making her breasts ache deliciously before he suckled them. With the flat of his hands, he rolled her remaining clothes down her body, kissing powder-soft skin as he exposed it, inch by inch. He slid lower, rolling his thumbs over the proud protrusions of her pelvic bones. He felt her stiffen against him.

"Relax, sweet Sarah," he urged, his voice low and soothing. "Share this with me, too. Let me show you how much I love you."

His voice came to Sarah through a haze of heat, intensifying as his mouth moved over her thighs, her abdomen, and into the hidden reaches of her womanhood, sending shock waves throughout her body. She called his name, and he rose above her on the strong pillars of his arms, dropping his head to answer near her ear, "I'm with you, Sarah."

"Be with me more," she pleaded. "Be with me now. Be part of me." He needed her. She felt the proof of his need and shifted her hips to welcome him, but he only lowered himself to his elbows and undulated against her.

"I will," he promised. "I'll be part of you even after I'm gone."

"I know."

"And you'll be part of me."

"I want you, Connor," she whispered desperately.

"I want you to love me," he insisted, his voice hoarse with the effort.

"I do. Oh, I do."

"Then say it. Say it now, while you need me more than the air you breathe."

"I love you, Connor. I love you." He slipped inside her, and she repeated the words as the pace of his thrusting escalated. With firm hands he rotated her hips toward himself, reaching to touch the deepest part of her. Her words became one soft, driven cry as she rose to meet him in shuddering mindless release.

Trembling, Connor rolled to his back. The power of his passion scared him. She'd said she would drive him wild, and she nearly had. But he'd managed to pace himself, and she'd trusted him and let herself go completely in his arms. If she could trust him in that, he had to believe she would trust him with her life someday—hers and Dannie's.

She stirred in his arms and rubbed her cheek against his shoulder. "Are you with me still?" he asked quietly.

"I don't want to fall asleep, not tonight." Her sigh echoed her contentment. "I want to stay awake and keep feeling this wonderful feeling."

"How do you feel?"

"Totally tranquilized. What did you give me?"

"Good loving."

"Mmm. If you could bottle it, you could make a fortune."

He drew her hair back from her forehead to find a spot for his kiss. "'I'm givin' my woman all I got,'" he whispered, quoting his own song.

"I wanted to work my wiles on you," she said. With one eye she watched her forefinger tunnel through the tufts of golden hair on his chest. "I wanted you to be senseless with passion, but somewhere along the line I sort of... lost the nerve."

His chest rumbled with his throaty chuckle. "You kept up the volley pretty well, though. You work your wiles on me every time you flash me that soulful, brown-eyed look of yours."

"I should have worn something black and filmy," she decided.

"Your big flannel shirt with paint in the plaid drives me crazy," he confided. "Especially when you wear it with those shapeless jeans. Ouch!" Her tug on his hair left his chest smarting.

"I never pretended to be glamorous," she pouted.

"I never asked for glamorous. I asked for Sarah."

"I love you, Connor. If you'll be patient with me, I want to make love to you the same way you make love to me."

He wanted that, too. He ached for it in every corner of his heart, but he shook his head regretfully. "First you have to love me the same way I love you. You have to be willing to take all the risks, Sarah."

Sarah's hand stilled. "Don't you believe I love you?"

"Not enough," he said, his voice nearly toneless.

Chapter Twelve

Sarah did fall asleep in Connor's arms, but he lay awake long after he'd made love to her a second time. He loved the feeling of having her close while she slept. It was an intimacy, and he wanted every one he could have with her. She was fast becoming an obsession with him.

He was beginning to feel that he was the more vulnerable of the two of them, and he'd decided long ago that such a predicament was too costly. He'd shored up his defenses beautifully. He could handle his parents, his friends, his fans in groups of five or five thousand, but he knew he'd met his match in the woman who lay in his arms. Strange as it seemed for such a delicate, feminine creature, she epitomized the strong, silent type. If there were such a thing as emotional football, she'd make a hell of a defensive end.

He had a yen for a cigarette, and he decided to indulge himself. Without making a sound, he put on his pants and closed the bedroom door behind him.

The living room was bright with light reflected off the snow outside. Only the click of his lighter offended the night's quiet. He went to the window. He loved the warmth of this house, the comfortable feeling of home, but he hated curtains. He wanted to be able to see out. Shoving the sheer fabric aside, he braced his bare shoulder against the window frame and sent a stream of smoke toward the ceiling.

There was a fresh blanket of snow on the lawn, and it looked as though there would be more before morning. But for now, all was still and white. It was one of those nights when winter wound a cocoon around the earth, and everything slept peacefully inside the white shell. This was one of the things he missed about having winter—this kind of night. There was a coziness that you couldn't have inside unless it was cold outside.

Coziness was a woman's word, he thought. It was the kind of thing women made. It was the pillows and the slipcovers and the wicker basket that held the mail. It was the way he felt when he looked at a painting Sarah had done. The professional decorator couldn't give his home that feeling, but Sarah could. Her very presence could bring that feeling. She was his white cocoon.

Sarah was a clear, placid pool in a Japanese garden. She was the peaceful place he craved, and he wanted desperately for her to let him in. She was afraid of him, though. She was afraid he'd bring the loudness, the bright lights, the fast pace of his world with him and spoil hers. And then, he knew, she saw him leaving her after some time and maybe some words had passed between them. She wasn't able to trust him beyond the present.

Sarah crept into the living room on noiseless feet. Connor's shirt was her nightgown, and an afghan from the closet was her robe. She'd come looking for him without thinking about it first, and when she saw him standing there against the window frame, her breath caught in her chest. He was beautiful. The long, tapering V of his back made a leisurely descent into the beltless pants that rode low on his hips. The night bathed his shoulders and the crown of his head in soft white light. He was magnificently sculpted and well displayed in the subtlety of night light.

She had to remember that by tomorrow night he would be gone. She was glad he'd gotten up. Even in her sleep she'd missed him, and she'd awakened when her body realized he was no longer next to her. She didn't want to waste this time sleeping. Sarah wanted to crystallize this moment, save it under her pillow and relive it whenever she missed him unbearably. After he was gone, she wouldn't think of where he was or what he was doing or whether he was ever reminded of her under his hot lights and his reverberating amplifiers. She would think of him here, on this night, in the cool quiet of her living room.

Connor sensed her presence and turned toward her slowly. His hand came up, and the cigarette became a red glow in the darkness. "You caught me," he said, his voice low and husky. "Don't tell the press. They'll say you drove me to it."

"They'll say you did it out of spite because you know I have no ashtrays. It'll be quite the scandal."

The cigarette was deposited in the fireplace to become another dying ember. "It's starting to snow again. Come watch it with me," he said. When she did, he gathered her under his arm and turned to the window. It was a sparse, soft-sift snow, the kind that heralded the Christmas season.

"I want you to call me when you've arranged for Dannie's testing," he told her. "I want to be here. There are enough colleges in the area. I'm sure you'll be able to make some contacts through them. When you're ready, I'll be here. And I want all the bills."

"You're very difficult when it comes to money, Connor Ryan."

"I know. And I'm going to continue to be difficult, so brace yourself."

Sarah watched the falling snowflakes, but she saw the hot tears of frustration in the face of a small child. "What if it's true, Connor? What if she has this learning-disability thing? She isn't as strong as you are. Her feelings are easily hurt, and if she goes to school and can't learn..."

He had her shoulders in his hands before he knew it, and he had no idea how harsh his face looked in the shadows. "Don't ever say she can't learn," he said slowly, forcing absolute calm into his voice.

"I meant...normally."

He drew a long breath and kept his voice low and steady. "What's normal, Sarah? What the hell is normal? Is your brother, Jerry, normal? How about your parents, or mine? Was Kevin the normal one in my family, and are you the normal one in yours?" He paused and eyed her narrowly.

She grabbed his arms, bracing her hands just above his elbows. "Connor, I only meant..."

"Normal doesn't exist, Sarah. I have looked high and low, and I can't find it. Everybody's above the bell curve in some ways and below it in others. I thank God I found that out before I drove myself crazy trying to squeeze into it."

"Maybe normal isn't the word I wanted, Connor. I meant... usual, ordinary, run-of-the-mill. That's what I understand. I'm a very average woman, an average artist, and I guess I wasn't prepared for anything but an average child."

"None of that is true, Sarah." The intensity was still bright in his eyes, but there was no longer any harshness. In his heart, he felt every word he said. "You are the most beautiful of women. You're a gifted artist. But those judgments are made by my standards, my values. Another man might..." He stopped himself, shaking his head. "Another man would be crazy not to agree with me, but then I have a lover's bias. And as for Dannie, she's still the same child you rightfully called precocious. That hasn't changed."

Of course it hadn't changed. Dannie was still Dannie, and they didn't know anything for sure, and even if she had this problem, it wasn't... Sarah's face filled with tears. "Connor, help me. I'm afraid I'm not up to it. You said she was more yours than Kevin's, and that's true, and I'm afraid she's more yours than..."

"No, Sarah." He pulled her into his arms and held her close, giving his bare skin to her tears. "Shh. You're her mother, and that will never change."

"But you understand...everything..."

"Of course I do. It's been with me for a long time."

"It's not just that. It's the way you see the world—so much the way Dannie does. I've watched you together. You're so much alike, I could almost swear..."

"So could I. Do you doubt Dannie's love for you, Sarah?" he asked gently.

"N-no."

"Then why do you doubt mine? Why are you afraid to love me as you love her? You'll adjust for her; you'll compromise as she grows, as all the changes come. Why are you so afraid to do the same for me?"

She waited to answer until she thought she could hold her voice steady. It came out as a rasp. "I *have* compromised for you, Connor. More than you know."

"I think I know. You've decided to let me play the stud for you. It isn't what I want, but if it's all I can have, I'll take it."

She drew back to look at him, astonished. "Let you play the..."

He gave her half a smile. "Did I step on your toes there? Would you have had it the other way around? You're the one who refuses to marry me, Sarah."

"But you're the one who's..."

"Let me tell you who I'm not. I'm not your father, who ran out on your mother for the greater glory of television. I'm not Kevin Ryan, who went down with his helicopter and up in a cloud of smoke. And I'm not the college-professor type, who'd be home every night by five to give you your regular peck on the cheek." She lowered her eyes, and he shook her once. "Look at me, Sarah. I'm not a freak. I'm an entertainer, yes, but I'm not some Jekyll-and-Hyde crazy who gets lit with the groupies every night on the road and then spends a few weeks with his ladylove between tours. I want a home and a family, just like your *normal* men. I want you and Dannie, Sarah. And I want you for my *wife*, not my playmate."

"Connor, you can't even be with us for Christmas," she reminded him.

"No man can promise he'll be there every Christmas. A man can only promise to do his best and ask the same of his family. You can't promise me forever, Sarah, but you can give me your love, starting now without exceptions."

"Oh, Connor, I do love you, but I can't..."

Groaning, he pulled her into his arms again. "Don't," he ground out. "Don't say, 'Connor, I love you, *but.*'"

"Connor, I love you," she whispered, holding him.

"Then will you marry me?"

He waited, but she said nothing more. He sighed, granting her the right to say no more for the moment. "Come sit with me for a while, then," he said, leading her to the couch. "Sit with me and hold me until morning. Tomorrow I'll have to go." The shuddering catch in her breathing was unmistakable. "But you'll make me one of those old-fashioned New England Christmas dinners first, won't you?"

"I was counting on it," she said in a small voice.

"So was I." He sat with her on the couch, and they held each other, sharing her afghan. "Dannie's going to be all right, Sarah. We'll take her lots of places, and we'll show her things. We'll let her learn with her hands, which we both know is the way she wants to come to know about the world. And it works. I think with my hands." She felt his fingers on her face and her breast at once, and she made a little gratified sound in her throat. "I think, 'My God, how lovely she is.'"

"Connor, could you . . . light some of the candles? I love candlelight."

He reached for the lighter he'd laid on the table and shifted it to his other hand. On the table behind them stood a squadron of candles, and he began lighting them, one by one. "Sarah," he began, hesitating on the name, "I've left something for you in an envelope under the tree. A gift for myself, really. I want you to come to Austin. I want you to be there in the audience for me."

"Connor . . ."

"I know Christmas is out of the question, but this is on the twenty-seventh. I want to look down front and see you there." She said nothing, and he knew she had not refused. *Understand what it means to me, Sarah. Understand what I'm asking you for.* "If you can't be there, then I want you to watch the show on TV. It's important to me."

He laid the lighter back on the table and looked at her in the candlelight. Filling their heads with the scent of bayberry, they closed the distance between them for a kiss.

Connor had seen to it that his presence would be felt on Christmas. Dannie had insisted on baking oatmeal cookies for Santa's reindeer. Her dollhouse was delivered to the house on Christmas Eve, and Sarah had less than an easy time getting her ready for church. The sleeve of her green dress had to be pulled over two fists full of small wooden chairs. They sat in the back pew of the wood-and-white New England-style church and listened to Christmas hymns, old favorites that generally brought Sarah a feeling of security and contentment. This Christmas, however, that feeling wouldn't come. The emptiness that was hammering at her inside drove the feeling out.

Red roses were delivered to Sarah, and she wondered how he'd gotten anyone to deliver flowers on Christmas Day. The card offered her his love, and for a moment she had that Christmas feeling. But she laid the card on the table and turned away, and the feeling was lost again.

On the twenty-sixth, Sarah cleaned Lavinia Porter's house, top to bottom. The only remaining disorder was a pile of boxes on the dining-room table, but Mrs. Porter had instructed Sarah to leave those there. They were gifts to be returned.

Gifts to be returned. The meaningless, obligatory exchange of merchandise at Christmastime had nothing to do with gift giving. One didn't return a gift from the heart of a loved one. Sarah smiled. Connor was such a wonderful gift giver. She saw the look he always had when he waited for a reaction to his gift, whether it be a serape or a song. He anticipated someone else's pleasure. He wanted to make people happy.

And then she remembered the envelope. Airline tickets were expensive, and she'd thought of returning it. She had to call him. As soon as she got home, she'd call and explain.

The envelope held two tickets, both dated December twenty-seventh. One was an airline ticket, and one was a concert ticket. There was nothing else. She tried the concert hall but was told, of course, that Connor Ryan was not available. That was that. No hotel, no way to reach him by phone. And he hadn't called her since he'd left. He'd left her only one way to reach him. She had to make a choice.

Sarah sat by the phone, lost in her thoughts. Dannie was watching the new television. Sarah had never been much for television, but she supposed, for Dannie, in limited doses... Eyes on the screen, Sarah did a double take. It was a beer commercial with a well-known baseball coach bantering over the bar with the boys. One of the "boys"—hardly a boy—was Tony Benedict, her father.

Sarah leaned forward, taking advantage of the few seconds she had to study him. It had been a long time since she'd seen him in color. He was almost as gray as the coach. In fact, Sarah probably knew that coach about as well as she knew the man with the amiable smile who slapped the coach on the back and offered him a beer. Her father? He was just a face on the screen.

Let me tell you who I'm not. I'm not your father.

Sarah had the phone in her hand before she had a plan in her head. "Jerry, I need a favor. I have to be gone for a couple of days."

She went directly from the airport to the auditorium. She'd dressed for the concert before she left home, trying her best for chic with a simple, soft wool-jersey dress in emerald green. The dress's line flattered her trim figure, and the shade of green enhanced her coloring. She'd done her hair up with some artful French braiding, and she wore pure white pearl accents. She'd brought nothing but what she could carry in her purse. It was the most delightfully impulsive traveling she'd ever done.

If she'd expected to be outclassed by a glamorous audience, she was to be disappointed. People were dressed casually in jeans and western clothes. She was directed to her seat by a man in a cowboy hat. In fact, there were lots of cowboy hats around, most of them looking as though they'd actually ridden the range and been stepped on a time or two by the wearer's horse. There were rows of tables near the stage, and behind them were semicircular tiers of bleachers. People were drinking beer out of quart-size paper cups and generally gearing up for a rollicking good time, the kind Georgia Nights could provide.

A table near the stage had been saved for Sarah, and on it lay a single long-stemmed rose. She brought it to her nose and breathed its sweetness, thinking how sad it would have been for this rose to lie here at an empty table. She was glad she'd come. He must have known she would.

He watched her smooth her dress beneath her legs before she sat down, and his heart thumped like one of Scotch's wild drum solos. She picked up the rose, and he could smell it himself. All of his senses told him that she was really here.

"See any pretty faces in the front row, my friend?"

The hand on Connor's shoulder and the concerned voice that went with it belonged to Scotch Hagan. Connor hadn't told Scotch, but it hadn't been necessary to tell him. Scotch knew what Connor was waiting for. Without taking his eyes off Sarah, Connor reported quietly, "Just one. The right one."

"Hot damn!" Scotch exclaimed, slapping Connor on the back. "Let's go out there and make that woman some music, boy!"

"Didn't you get a beer, ma'am?" An older man in a western-cut three-piece suit leaned over toward Sarah from the next table. His Southern drawl and his friendly smile were both genuine. He was with an attractive brunette, who also offered Sarah a smile.

"No, I didn't."

"Would you like one? I'll get it for you."

"No, thank you."

"How far did you come for the show tonight?" the woman asked. No doubt Sarah sounded as out of place as she probably looked.

"Light-years," she said, and then added with a smile, "I'm from Massachusetts."

"You know someone?" the woman asked, tipping her head toward the stage. Sarah nodded, the pride showing in her eyes. "Connor Ryan?" the woman wondered.

"Yes. How did you know?"

"I'm Maggie Hagan, Scotch's wife. This is Scotch's daddy."

The man nodded, still smiling. "Wilbur Hagan," he offered.

"Come join us, Sarah," Maggie invited. "Scotch told me all about you. Connor should have told us you were coming instead of sitting you over there all by yourself. Of course, the minute I saw you, I knew who you were."

"He didn't really know himself, not for sure."

Maggie's eyes lit up with the prospect of witnessing Connor's surprise. "Then won't he be pleased!"

The warm-up was a flashy sister act, two whiskey-voiced women with hair the color of cotton who were dressed in similar sequin-spangled black outfits. Their voices blended like a perfectly mixed Manhattan, and they went down smoothly with the audience, bringing the crowd up to a titillated pitch. The crowd was ready for Georgia Nights and Sarah was right with them. The stage was set, and the butterflies in Sarah's stomach were for Connor.

"Ladies and gentlemen—Georgia Nights!"

The crowd went wild as the four appeared on stage one after another—Scotch taking his place behind the drums, Kenny Rasmussen bounding to the far end to pick up his bass guitar, Connor taking his place on the side where Sarah sat and Mike Tanner coming on last to claim center stage.

Connor gave his eyes a moment to adjust to the light as the band launched right into its favorite opener, "Summer Nights in Georgia." The tempo was upbeat, and Connor felt it slither along his spine and down to his knees as he rolled with it. The minute he saw faces down the front, he looked for Sarah. The table was empty, and the rose was gone. He tucked his chin to the left and watched his fingers dance over the guitar neck's frets as though absolutely nothing was wrong. She'd been there. Maybe someone had offended her—spilled beer on her dress or something. He glanced back out and found Maggie's table, and his stomach somersaulted as he swung into the chorus.

Sarah knew the moment he saw her. He didn't miss a beat, but his blue eyes lit up like Roman candles, and she felt her face burn with the heat they gave off. She was radiant. He soared.

Connor was a professional, and he played to the audience, but he played for Sarah. On a bluegrass number he made a banjo come alive and chatter nonstop at the dependable guitars. His fiddle brought the Smoky Mountains to Texas, and the bleachers clattered with foot stomping. Even Mike Tanner was amazed as the crowd roared its approval.

"Y'all kinda like that fiddle?" Applause was the enthusiastic reply. "How long can you keep 'em stompin' like that, Connor?"

"Till the roof caves in," Connor promised, swinging into an encore on the fiddle.

Sarah became part of the crowd. She clapped and tapped and even shouted her approval once or twice. Every time she caught his eye, he grinned. He was on top of the world.

"Ladies and gentlemen," Mike said, wiping a sleeve across his glistening forehead. "Georgia Nights is proud to introduce a new song tonight, one that'll be featured

on our next album. It's a song that Connor Ryan wrote,
and one that only Connor can sing. He's about to show
you why.''

The stage lights were cut momentarily, and the white
spotlight singled Connor out as he settled on a stool
with a twelve-string guitar. He found Sarah in the
darkness and announced huskily, as though only for
her, ''This is 'Sarah's Song.''' With backup from the
rest of the band he sang:

You came to me in a whispered moment
When the crowd roared in my head
You gave me peace instead
And I knew love.

You came to me in the halo of the moon
When the sun had seared my eyes
You gave me no more lies
You gave me love.

You came to me on a wishful thought
In a palette of pastel
The face I love so well
And you saw me as I was
And you took me as I was
And gave your love.

Oh, Sarah, the touch of your hand, my Sarah
Just one kiss, my Sarah
And I can't let you go
Don't ask that of me, Sarah,
I can never let you go.

The stage went dark, and the audience was stunned. Sarah closed her eyes and let two tears roll down her cheeks. Applause thundered behind her, but the darkness gave her a few seconds' privacy. The song was hers, her gift from Connor's heart. Sensing sudden light, she took a quick swipe at the tears with trembling hands.

Connor took advantage of the dark seconds to hop down from the stage. He sidestepped a security guard and reached for Sarah just as the house lights came on. Pulling her from her seat, he saw her surprise, and he answered it with a quick, joy-filled kiss. There was a scattering of applause nearby, but the joyous roar in Sarah's ears blocked out all but Connor.

"It was beautiful," she whispered.

"So are you." He kissed her again, gently, as befitted a thing of beauty.

"Way to go, cowboy!" someone shouted.

Sarah's eyes widened. "Connor, all these people..."

Grinning at her, Connor confided, "I'm from Waco tonight. They're just giving the hometown boy a little encouragement."

He was pulling her toward a curtain while the security guard, tossing Connor an appreciative wink, ran interference with a small group of fans. Sarah found herself tucked in a small, dimly lit corner, a wall at her back and folds of blue curtain on either side. "Is this a break?" she asked.

He couldn't stop grinning. "Yeah, and I'm dying of thirst." His hands snatched her at the waist and brought her hard against him. Sarah dropped her head back as his mouth descended, this time in blatant hunger. He kissed her again and again, and she rose on tiptoe, fastening her arms over his shoulders, feeling the dampness of his shirt through her dress.

Raising his head at last he sighed with relief. "God, you taste good." Then he dove in for another kiss.

Laughing, Sarah tipped her head back. "Connor, you're in the middle of a concert."

"We've got fifteen minutes," he growled, settling for a ripe spot on her neck. "Sally Bridger has a solo here, and then she does a number with Mike."

"Who's Sally Bridger?"

"An up-and-coming country star." His spreading hands pulled her hips tight against his, and he gave her a hot-eyed smile. "In case you haven't noticed, babe, so am I."

Sarah feigned shock. "On national television, Mr. Ryan?"

"This is where the guitar comes in real handy." She laughed at that, and he looked at her, shaking his head and smiling as though she'd just performed an incredible feat. "You're here, Sarah. I can't believe it."

"You knew I'd come."

"I've never done so much hoping and praying, lady. I was afraid I'd backed you into a corner and lost you because of it."

Sarah glanced first to one side, then the other. "You've got me in a corner now. I don't see an escape." Her hands tightened at the back of his neck. "I want to take the risks, Connor. I love you."

He kissed her again, deeply and possessively. She wanted to be his, and she was willing to be part of his life, the best and the worst of it. His kiss reassured her that he was worth the risks. When he drew back, they heard applause. Their eyes met, and they laughed together.

"Let's go to the hotel," he urged in a husky voice.

"But the show must go on." Sarah's eyes danced as Connor rolled his skyward.

"I can see you're going to be one of those pushy stage wives. Tell you what. I'll go back out and give 'em 'Misty River Morning,' and they'll have to be satisfied."

Sarah shook her head. "I wouldn't be satisfied. I'd want my money back."

"That's why the encore's just for you." He slid his hands up her back and tightened his hold.

"Really?"

"I'm taking you back to the hotel..." He was nuzzling her ear.

"Mmm-hmm?"

"As soon as this is over..."

She felt a little nip at her earlobe, and she giggled. "And?"

"And I'm gonna do one hell of a job with 'Givin' My Woman All I Got.' "

Sarah smiled and whispered, "Let's hurry up and get to the encore."

Silhouette Special Edition

COMING NEXT MONTH

CHEROKEE FIRE—Gena Dalton
It was Sabrina Dante's silver spoon that Cherokee cowboy Jarod Redfeather couldn't trust. The two lovers came from opposite worlds, but the Indian heritage taught them to overcome their differences.

A FEW SHINING HOURS—Jeanne Stephens
Fifteen years ago, Quinn left for Vietnam, not knowing about the daughter he had given Kathleen. Now he was back, hoping that love could make time stand still.

PREVIEW OF PARADISE—Tracy Sinclair
Travis couldn't resist rescuing Bettina from being sold at an auction by nomad chieftains. But a valuable amulet had been stolen, and his damsel in distress was the number one suspect!

A PASSIONATE ILLUSION—Tory Cates
Tempers flared when Matthew accused Lissa of not being able to act. He wanted her to bring illusion alive with passion—passion as real as the hunger he could no longer deny...

ALL MY LOVE, FOREVER—Pamela Wallace
They were adults now—not lovestruck teenagers. But even after the hurt of raising their child alone, Carolyn still loved Rafe. She only knew she wanted him...more than ever before.

FORWARD PASS—Brooke Hastings
Federal drug agent Liz Reynolds never intended to win a trip to Hawaii with star quarterback Zack Delaney. But now Zack was in for the most challenging game of his career.

AVAILABLE THIS MONTH:

RIGHT BEHIND THE RAIN
Elaine Camp

SPECIAL DELIVERY
Monica Barrie

PRISONER OF LOVE
Maranda Catlin

GEORGIA NIGHTS
Kathleen Eagle

FOCUS ON LOVE
Maggi Charles

ONE SUMMER
Nora Roberts

Take 4 Silhouette Romance novels
FREE

Then preview 6 brand-new Silhouette Romance® novels—delivered to your door as soon as they are published—for 15 days without obligation. When you decide to keep them, pay just $1.95 each, *with no shipping, handling or other charges of any kind!*

Each month, you'll meet lively young heroines and share in their thrilling escapades, trials and triumphs... virile men you'll find as attractive and irresistible as the heroines do... and colorful supporting characters you'll feel you've always known.

Start with 4 Silhouette Romance novels absolutely FREE. They're yours to keep without obligation, and you can cancel at any time.

As an added bonus, you'll also get the Silhouette Books Newsletter FREE with every shipment. Every issue is filled with news on upcoming books, interviews with your favorite authors, even their favorite recipes.

Simply fill out and return the coupon today!
This offer is not available in Canada.

Silhouette Books, 120 Brighton Rd., P.O. Box 5084, Clifton, NJ 07015-5084

AMERICAN
TRIBUTE

American Tribute titles now available:

RIGHT BEHIND THE RAIN
Elaine Camp #301—April 1986
The difficulty of coping with her brother's
death brought reporter Raleigh Torrence
to the office of Evan Younger, a police
psychologist. He helped her to deal with
her feelings and emotions, including love.

THIS LONG WINTER PAST
Jeanne Stephens #295—March 1986
Detective Cody Wakefield checked out
Assistant District Attorney Liann McDowell,
but only in his leisure time. For it was the
danger of Cody's job that caused Liann to
shy away.

LOVE'S HAUNTING REFRAIN
Ada Steward #289—February 1986
For thirty years a deep dark secret kept them
apart—King Stockton made his millions while
his wife, Amelia, held everything together.
Now could they tell their secret, could they
admit their love?

Take 4 Silhouette Special Edition novels
FREE

and preview future books in your home for 15 days!

When you take advantage of this offer, you get 4 Silhouette Special Edition® novels FREE and without obligation. Then you'll also have the opportunity to preview 6 brand-new books —delivered right to your door for a FREE 15-day examination period—as soon as they are published.

When you decide to keep them, you pay just $1.95 each ($2.50 each in Canada) *with no shipping, handling, or other charges of any kind!*

Romance *is* alive, well and flourishing in the moving love stories of Silhouette Special Edition novels. They'll awaken your desires, enliven your senses, and leave you tingling all over with excitement . . . and the first 4 novels are yours to keep. You can cancel at any time.

As an added bonus, you'll also receive a FREE subscription to the Silhouette Books Newsletter as long as you remain a member. Each issue is filled with news on upcoming books, interviews with your favorite authors, even their favorite recipes.

To get your 4 FREE books, fill out and mail the coupon today!

Silhouette Special Edition®

Silhouette Books, 120 Brighton Rd., P.O. Box 5084, Clifton, NJ 07015-5084